MW00653209

SPLIT SECONDS

KIMBERLEE MAJKSZAK

Copyright © 2018 by Kimberlee Majkszak

All rights reserved. This book or any portion thereof
may not be reproduced or used in any manner whatsoever
without the express written permission of the publisher
except for the use of brief quotations in a book review.

Printed in the United States

Print ISBN: 978-1-7327029-1-2
eBook ISBN: 978-1-7327029-0-5

Cover and interior design by TeaBerryCreative.com

To Wayne
Whose faith never wavered and whose
Encouragement never faltered

CHAPTER 1

KADEN LICKED THE ICE CREAM FROM HER FINGERS. The chocolate liquid dripped down the cone and Kaden's pink tongue followed its trail. She examined her mound of remaining ice cream for a moment then took another lick. Her attention was captured by a commotion over by the water.

"Mommy, look at the gooses." Kaden's little face broke out in a grin. "They want to eat the grass."

Georgia smiled at her daughter. "When it's more than one you call them geese."

"Oh," Kaden looked thoughtful then proudly said, "The geeses are eating the grass."

Georgia laughed and hugged Kaden to her. She loved these spring days when the air was fresh and clean. She took a deep breath. The sky was so blue overhead without a cloud in sight. The first flowers to poke their blooms out were so bright after the dreary days of winter that Georgia's spirits were lifted just to see them.

She and Kaden came here at least twice a week until the summer heat became too intense. July and August in the Texas summer consisted of an hour in the neighborhood swimming pool and the rest of the day indoors. But for the brief time it lasted, there was nothing to compare to a spring day in Central Texas.

Kaden's chocolate ice cream dripped from her cone into the dirt at their feet, a drop or two landing on her pink Minnie Mouse tee shirt. Georgia made a mental note to pretreat before the laundry basket but the day was too beautiful to care about stains on tee shirts and rips in jeans. She was the kind of mom, anyway, who enjoyed Kaden's childhood, and she was easygoing about things she didn't consider important to Kaden's development. She wanted her child to have a happy childhood, filled with memories of all the fun times they shared. That was what would shape Kaden's personality for the best, thought Georgia. She would grow up happy and confident, at ease with who she was in this world. At barely five years old, there was plenty of time to catch up on learning about the hard things in life.

Kaden wiped her sticky hands on her pants leg while her mom wasn't looking. She looked around the little park that she secretly thought of as her own personal playground, trying to decide what to do next.

"Mommy, will you push me on the swing?"

Georgia looked at her watch and knew they should head home, but Kaden was already grabbing her hand to pull her toward the swings.

"Kaden, we only have time for a short swing, okay? Daddy will be home for dinner soon."

Kaden jumped up on the swing and held on, her long blonde hair blowing behind her and her legs dangling under her. "Ok, Mommy, but push me high!"

Georgia took her place behind the swing and gently pushed, watching to make sure Kaden held on with both hands. Sometimes it was hard to believe how happy she was with this life of trips to the park, playing Barbie, and baking cookies. Georgia had worked for many years as an office assistant at an architectural firm and she enjoyed her career. But nothing had prepared her for the contentment she found once she and Ryan had started their own family.

At the age of 29, Georgia had been married for 6 years and she was ready to start a family. They happily waited for the positive pregnancy results each month but a year passed and it still had not happened. Months of trying to get pregnant followed by increasing desperation with each negative test. Georgia became depressed. She felt like a failure. Ryan accepted things in stride but he wanted Georgia to be happy. Finally, they had gone to a fertility clinic for help. The tests, the injections and timing were nearly impossible to manage. The mood swings and depression with each passing month and a negative test result drove both of them to the brink of divorce. They were nearly at the end of their financial ability and things were tense in the household. It was only because Georgia had finally taken drastic steps that they even had Kaden. A spontaneous frown appeared on

3

Georgia's face as she thought of the secret she still kept from Ryan. She knew it wasn't the right thing to do. She knew it was dangerous. *We had to do something*, she told herself again, and it was worth it a thousand times over. Georgia shook herself out of her memories and concentrated on Kaden's laughter as she kicked her legs in the air. It was worth whatever the cost.

Giving one last push, she sent the swing a little higher to Kaden's appreciative shriek of joy. The swing gently slowed and came to a rest.

"Come on, Kaden, we really have to go. Daddy will be home soon and you know how hungry he gets."

"Like a big ol' bear" Kaden chimed in, knowing this story well.

"That's right, just like a big old bear and we want to make sure dinner is ready so he doesn't eat us up."

Kaden giggled and hopped off the swing as Georgia stepped over to their bench and started to gather their things. She waved to a couple of other moms she knew and then held out her hand to Kaden.

"Come on, Butterfly, let's go." With their satchel of snacks in one hand and Kaden chattering happily at her side, Georgia let go of Kaden's hand to dig the car keys from her purse.

"Look, Mommy, balloons!" Kaden started running toward a bunch of red, blue, and gold balloons tied to a rock right beside the parking lot.

Georgia, still fumbling with her bag, finally got her hand on the key and looked up. With a sudden premonition she felt her heart seize and stop beating for a brief moment. Her voice sounded faint and far away and she couldn't seem to get air into her lungs. "Kaden, stop!"

Kaden hesitated, looked back at her mother, and waved her hand. The balloons dipped and waved in a slight breeze. The temptation was too much, and she turned back to the balloons and ran to the edge of the parking lot.

Georgia felt like a thick fog enveloped her as she watched Kaden reach out for a red balloon. Just as she pulled the string toward her there was a blur of movement as the driver of a beige sedan suddenly gunned the engine and the car lurched forward. The roar of the engine was deafening. It filled Georgia's head as she dropped her bags and opened her mouth to scream a warning that was already too late. The car headed directly for Kaden, seeming to target her. There was no last minute screech of brakes, no swerve to the side of the road. The impact of the hit seemed noiseless as the car reared up over the slight curb. Georgia watched as her daughter's small body was thrown into the air. For a brief moment, it floated like one of the balloons before, with a sickening thud, Kaden's crumpled shape landed on the pavement.

"No!" The scream that wrenched itself from Georgia made the two other mothers in the parking lot jerk with fear. Instinctively, they caught sight of their own children playing on the slide before running to Georgia. They saw a car speeding out of the park as a lone red balloon drifted up with the wind currents higher into the sky.

By the time the women reached the parking lot, Georgia was holding Kaden's unconscious, limp body in her arms, rocking back and forth as she whispered one word over and over. "No, no, no, no." Other than scrapes on her arms and legs, one of which stuck out at an odd angle, the only blood seemed to come from Kaden's mouth. Georgia kept wiping the bright redness from her face; soon her own hands and arms were red. Kaden didn't make a sound.

CHAPTER 2

THE AMBULANCE TOOK FOUR MINUTES and thirty-seven seconds to arrive. To Georgia it was a lifetime. She cradled Kaden to her chest, her arms wrapped tight around her. She had no awareness of anything or anyone else.

The other mothers stood by helplessly, Georgia's grief already washing over them as they silently thanked whatever Gods there were this was not their child.

They heard the sirens first, shattering the stillness of the morning. Then they saw the red and blue lights flashing through the trees. The other mothers, Amy and Robyn, moved toward Georgia as the ambulance screeched to a stop and the EMTs jumped out.

Amy took hold of Georgia's shoulders and pulled her up as Robyn gently unwound her arms from around Kaden.

"Honey the ambulance is here. We have to let them help her." Robyn's voice was gentle and compassionate. "Can we call someone for you?"

Georgia's body stiffened at the touch of these two women, who a moment ago, had been comrades, confidants, mothers all sharing commonality. As she looked at Kaden's body, limp and lifeless, Georgia already felt different from them. She tried to remember a few minutes ago when Kaden's blue eyes had sparkled with delight and her laugh had floated on the air. She tried to remember Kaden's voice when it called her mommy. Now Kaden's eyes were closed and her tiny chest barely moved with her effort to breathe. Georgia's frantic eyes never left Kaden's face as she tried to memorize everything about her. The EMTs finally arrived and started probing Kaden, setting up an IV, asking about medications, allergies, and if she'd been conscious. Georgia couldn't find words to answer any of the questions.

She could feel Amy put an arm around her shoulders but she shook her off. Robyn asked her something but she couldn't seem to understand the words. She was desperately trying to hear the EMTs and make sense of what they were saying. It seemed as if they were speaking another language. Nothing made sense to her as long as Kaden wasn't opening her eyes to look at her.

Finally, Robyn stood directly in front of Georgia, blocking her view of the medical team. Her voice was firm now. "Listen to me. Who can I call for you?"

Her attention snapped to Robyn at the question and Georgia understood they were trying to help her. "My phone—in the bag—Ryan," she whispered.

"Got it," Robyn hurried across the playground to Georgia's bags, dropped to the ground and started to gather the spilled contents. She found the phone and scrolled to find Ryan's number.

The EMTs were loading Kaden onto a stretcher and the police had arrived. Georgia's only thought was for her daughter and she turned to Amy.

"Can you take care of this for me?" She pleaded.

"Go." Amy pushed her a little toward the open back door of the ambulance. "We'll find you."

Georgia ran forward and took Kaden's hand, squeezing it, hoping for a response, as the EMTs loaded the stretcher.

"Baby, baby, it's Mommy. I'm with you, baby. Don't be scared." She hopped into the ambulance with Kaden, the EMT slammed the door and they were off.

Amy turned to Robyn who still had the phone to her ear, on hold for Ryan. Both women had blood on their clothes and a desperate hope in their hearts that their instinct was wrong and the little girl would be okay.

CHAPTER 3

STRIDING DOWN THE HALL, Ryan Maxwell looked around for someone to help him.

Finally, he saw at the far end of the hall a desk with an Information sign. He didn't wait for the woman to look up when he got to the desk.

"I need to find my daughter."

The urgency in his tone of voice got through to the woman, an experienced volunteer at St. Luke's for many years. She recognized panic and fear in the man's voice and didn't take his brusqueness personally.

"Let me put you on hold a moment please" she said into the phone, then looked up at the dark- haired man before her. He had a handsome face and was in good physical shape, but right now his brown eyes were full of questions and worry creased his forehead.

"What is your daughter's name, sir?"

"Kaden Renae Maxwell," Ryan made an effort to take a deep breath to calm himself down, but he couldn't seem to be able to get any air into his lungs. "She was brought in by ambulance."

"Okay, that's helpful. Let's see if she was admitted." The woman thumbed through her computer screens, then picked up the phone. Connecting a free line, she spoke quickly and efficiently. Her face betrayed nothing as she listened to the response, although her eyes flicked up quickly to Ryan's face. Then she smiled at him as she replied to the phone receiver.

"Okay, I have the father here. I'll get him down to you."

She turned back to Ryan who was trying not to show his impatience as he shifted his feet from side to side. Taking the directions to the ER, Ryan thanked her and broke into a half run as he headed to the elevator. The volunteer's smile faded as she sighed and turned back to her phones.

The ping of the elevator doors had barely sounded when Ryan was through them and face to face with a frosted glass enclosure with a sign that read "Family." He was about to turn back to the hall when he saw Georgia, huddled into herself, small and quiet in the corner of the room.

She had ignored the chairs and sat on the floor holding her knees tight into her chest with her eyes closed, her lips moving in a silent prayer. Her blonde hair was tucked behind her ears and her face was tear stained. There was blood smeared across her shirt. Ryan's breath caught in his throat as he realized it was his little girl's blood.

12

He crossed the room in three steps and kneeled in front of her, touching her shoulder gently.

Georgia's eyes popped open and she stared at Ryan as if she didn't recognize him.

Then tears filled her eyes, running down her checks, as she lifted her arms to him as if she were a child. Ryan quickly held her to him and stood up. Slowly he guided them to a small sofa.

In bits and pieces, Georgia's story came out. She told Ryan every detail she could remember, reliving the events of the day with him. Finally, there was nothing else to say or do except wait for the doctor's appearance. Exhausted by her emotions, Georgia laid her head against Ryan's chest. Comforted by his arm around her shoulders, she fell into a troubled sleep.

Ryan saw the weariness in the doctor as he approached. He was young, not much older than Ryan. He probably had kids the same age. In another life he and Ryan might have been friends at their kids' soccer games or a PTA meeting. But in this life, this man held Ryan's world in his hands. Something inside of Ryan broke as he looked into the doctor's face.

Rousing Georgia from sleep, Ryan shook hands with the physician and started to stand. The doctor motioned him to remain on the sofa and took a nearby chair himself. Beside him, Georgia was instantly alert.

"Mr. and Mrs. Maxwell, I'm Dr. Abbott, pediatric surgeon on staff here at St. Luke's. Your daughter suffered internal injuries in the accident as well as a concussion and broken leg. After stabilizing the leg, we performed surgery to stop the internal bleeding. Unfortunately, the impact of the accident caused a chest injury that tore the aorta. The damage was massive. Despite our best efforts, I am truly sorry to say that we were not able to save your daughter. She passed away on the operating table a few minutes ago."

Ryan put his head in his hands trying to absorb the news. Georgia sat absolutely still beside him for several seconds then she suddenly jumped to her feet. Her face was red and her eyes angry.

"What are you telling me?" she screamed at the doctor. "How can that be true?

You're lying! You're lying! You have to be lying!"

Dr. Abbott remained seated and looked at her calmly. "I wish I were, Mrs. Maxwell. I truly do. Please believe me when I tell you we tried everything we could to save your little girl. The accident damaged the chest cavity severely.

There was an aortic tear creating internal hemorrhaging."

Ryan's eyes were red and his hands shook but his voice was steady. "Did she suffer?"

Dr. Abbot's gaze lingered on Georgia still standing in front of him, her body rigid and hands clinched at her sides. Then he turned to Ryan.

"No, she didn't regain consciousness. I'll be happy to go over with you in more detail at a later time if questions come up." He handed Ryan a card. "I am truly sorry."

As he got up to leave, Georgia started forward and grabbed Dr. Abbott's arm.

"Just tell me it's a mistake, okay? I won't be mad. I promise. It's just a mistake, right?"

"I'm sorry, Mrs. Maxwell." Dr. Abbott gently untangled his arm from her grasp and with a last look at Ryan he left the consult room.

Georgia turned to her husband. "Ryan?" her voice was full of fear, confusion and desperation. As the truth hit her Georgia sank to her knees on the floor. Ryan knelt with her and held her tightly as they both wept.

CHAPTER 4

PUSHING ASIDE THE PLATTER loaded with fried chicken, Georgia set the spaghetti casserole on the table. Plastering a smile on her face she turned to her next door neighbor, Gwen.

Gwen's expression held the same look of concern that Georgia had seen a hundred times in the last few days. She reached out to pat Georgia's arm and said, "We're here for you, Georgia. If you need anything you should call."

"Thank you so much Gwen"

Georgia felt like she was going to slap Gwen if she didn't get away from her and her sympathy. Gwen had no idea what it felt like and how empty Georgia's house was now. Georgia knew she would never eat a bite of all this food but it was what people did at times like this to feel that they were helping in some way. It took all of Georgia's self- control to not start screaming that more food was not going to help. It wasn't going to take away the horrible, painful emptiness that consumed her. Walking Gwen back through to the living room, Georgia finally closed the door and leaned against it. A part of her knew people were sincere and trying to help but she felt like she could not endure one more hug, one more sad smile or pat on the shoulder. She sighed and listened to the silence in the house. Ryan had gone to the gym. Again. It was a way for him to get away from the sadness for a few minutes and Georgia felt her jealousy bubble up.

She couldn't leave the house. She was angry that Ryan could move on with his life. This was the only place she could still feel Kaden with her. She involuntarily glanced to her left up the quiet stairs, half expecting to see Kaden sleepily making her way down to the playroom. When she woke from her nap she would sit on the stairs and wiggle her bottom onto the next step until she reached the end of the stairs or fell back asleep. Sometimes as Georgia watched her slowly inching along Kaden would lean against the balustrade and her eyes would flutter close as she cuddled up on the stair.

The soft knock on the door behind her back startled Georgia back into the present and she raised shaking hands to her face. Wiping her face dry, she took a deep breath to push aside the anger at being called away from her memory. She prepared her plastic face- mask to accept another casserole from another sympathetic neighbor. She opened the door and quickly found herself enveloped in a hug so tight it took her breath. Clouds of auburn brown hair smelling of vanilla surrounded her. Georgia held on to her best friend and hugged her back as the tears returned.

Caroline held on to her friend's shoulder and looked at Georgia's face. Her blue eyes filled with tears as she steered Georgia back into the house.

"Oh, Honey. I am so sorry. Is Ryan here? What can I do?" The flurry of questions and activity coming from Caroline stunned Georgia into silence as the first real smile she had smiled in days appeared.

"I'm just glad you're here. I can't believe you're here."

Caroline threw her bag on the sofa and took charge. "Have you eaten anything? No, I didn't think so. Let's see what we've got."

She steered Georgia to the kitchen, sat her in a chair and started peeking into dishes. Within minutes Georgia had a small plate in front of her with chicken salad, slices of tomato, and a fresh roll.

"Now try to eat a little okay? I know you don't want to but you will need to keep your energy later. Do you want to tell me about what happened?"

Picking at her food with her fork, Georgia told her story again. Caroline had heard it but it helped Georgia to talk out the details. Each time she told the story Georgia saw it a little clearer. She was certain that the driver of the car had seen Kaden. The driver had sped up and moved toward her. Even if somehow they didn't see her, why didn't they stop? Why were the balloons left in the parking lot anyway? It was a sure thing some child from the park would be enticed by balloons. Who could do such a thing?

Caroline listened until Georgia had no more words. She had actually eaten most of her chicken salad when she finished talking and felt better. But she still had no answers.

Finally, they both fell silent. The afternoon was turning to evening but they sat in the darkening room, nursing cups of tea in big mugs.

"You never told me where Ryan is? Is he handling things okay? Shouldn't he be home?"

Georgia stirred her tea thoughtfully before answering. "He's at the gym. He's been at the gym a lot lately. It helps him." She took a deep breath and turned away from Caroline before continuing. "I think... I mean, I wonder... Caroline, what if this is all my fault? I never told him! I let us live with this lie for years and never told him. Maybe this is somehow my fault."

"What, some kind of cosmic pay back? I don't believe things work like that, not for one second. Your little girl was the victim of a horrible accident but it had nothing to do with you."

"But I should have told him. Not just about the money but everything. I should have told him about Kaden."

The sound of the garage door opening stopped Georgia but the panic she felt remained in her eyes.

"Caroline," she warned. "He doesn't know. Be careful what you say."

The back door swung open and Ryan wearily tossed his gym bag down. He saw Caroline and headed over to hug her as Caroline stood. "Ryan, I'm so sorry," she whispered.

"Sorry about the gym and all that. Good to see you Caroline. Glad you're here." He turned away and flicked on low lights near the cabinets before looking at Georgia, assessing her state of mind. Hesitantly he bent over and kissed her cheek. His own face was drawn and there were circles under his eyes. "How are you doing babe?"

"It's better with Caroline here." Georgia's voice was friendly but there was a distance in her manner toward Ryan.

"Let me grab a quick shower then we'll see about dinner, okay?"

Caroline watched Ryan go down the hall and heard the soft click of the bedroom door.

"Georgia, I know this is tough for you both but is something else happening here? I've never seen you so polite to your husband."

Georgia's shoulders slumped. "It's not him, it's me. I feel so guilty. I was the one with her when it happened. It was my job to keep her safe. He hasn't said so but he must blame me. I failed all of us. I feel like I killed her."

Caroline knelt beside her friend. "Oh, Georgia! It isn't your fault. He knows that you aren't to blame."

"Really? Are you sure about that? And how do you think he would feel if I told him the truth? Do you think he would understand if he knew he isn't Kaden's natural father? Do you think he would blame me then?"

CHAPTER 5

RYAN ROLLED OVER TO FIND the bed beside him empty. Night was just giving way to day. He patted the pillow next to him then as his eyes adjusted to the dawn's light he saw Georgia sitting by the window. Her legs were curled under her in the chair with Kaden's Hello Kitty blanket over her. Ryan rubbed his eyes and lay in bed a moment thinking about what was in store today. Finally, he threw back the covers and stumbled over to his wife. "Babe, you okay?"

Georgia didn't look up at him but reached out and took his hand. Bringing it to her mouth she kissed the back of his hand.

"I'm gonna hit the shower okay? It's getting late." Ryan squeezed her hand before heading to the bathroom. Georgia sat for a moment longer letting her mind wander through her memories of a life that was no longer hers then gathered herself together to head for the kitchen. The smell of freshly brewed coffee hit her nose and her appetite responded in spite of herself.

"I can't believe you are already awake after last night" She greeted Caroline with a hug. Caroline's auburn hair was tied back in a blue ribbon. It reminded Georgia of the color of Kaden's blue eyes and she tried to push the memory from her mind quickly, before she lost complete control of herself.

"Come on and sit," Caroline instructed as she put a cup of steaming hot coffee in front of Georgia. "I found some muffins. I'll warm them up. Is that okay for breakfast?"

"Its fine," Georgia let the steam from her cup warm her face as she cradled the mug. "We have to be at the service by 9:30. People will start arriving around then I'm sure. I just dread this, Caroline, all the hugging and pats on the back." She shuddered at the thought.

"I know, sweetie. People mean well though. Why don't you just signal me if you feel yourself about to lose it and I'll come to the rescue? Today you get to feel however you feel and not worry about other people."

"I'm sorry we talked so late last night but I really needed it. I'm just so glad you're here. I don't know if I could get through this without you." Georgia gratefully sipped from her mug. "Coffee's good."

"I've learned a few things over the years, my friend. How to make a good cup of coffee, and," Caroline shot a quick look at Georgia as she sat the warm muffins on the table before continuing, "when to be honest and trust those I love."

Georgia's eyes met Caroline's over the top of the cup. "I wish I could tell him. I really do, but it's too late now. I don't think it matters anymore."

"But it does, Georgia. Don't you see how keeping a secret like this will affect your entire relationship? You need to tell him."

"I don't know. I just don't think I can, especially now. It's what I tried to explain last night. He'll never understand. Maybe if I had told him before but the time was never right and now I don't think it will ever be right again. How can I take Kaden away from him all over again now?"

Caroline had no answer and all she could do was hug her friend's shoulder.

"I wish I had the answers for you. I really do. But I think he needs to know."

"Do you remember when we first met him? In Professor Greenhaw's class?"

Caroline smiled and looked at Georgia. "He was such a geek, wasn't he? But you knew right away there was something different about him. Even with his slicked back hair and socks that didn't match! I couldn't believe it when you told me after class that you were going to get him to ask you out."

"He was so shy and nervous. I don't think he could believe a girl was talking to him. But he was so sweet." "Well, it didn't take long for him to get the idea. I look at Ryan now and he's such a great guy. You really found a winner Georgia. And I think he's loved you from the first day you met. He deserves your trust."

Caroline leaned over the counter and held Georgia's hand. "It might be hard at first, but trust in him, Georgia."

Straightening as Ryan entered the kitchen, she gave a final squeeze of encouragement to Georgia. "Good morning," she greeted him with a cautious smile. "Let me get you some coffee."

"That would be great," Ryan kissed Georgia on the forehead as she half turned away. His unshaved cheek brushed against hers. "Is there any milk?"

Caroline busied herself with getting a mug, pouring the coffee, and setting out the milk while Ryan sat at the table with Georgia. He reached out a hand and took hers gently.

"I can't believe we have to do this."

"I know."

"We'll get through it together, Georgia. It's the only way we can do this."

The rest of the morning was a blur as they finished breakfast and prepared for the short drive to the memorial service. The phone had started ringing around 8:00 that morning and Caroline answered as many calls as she could until she turned the ringer off and let everything go to voicemail.

Finally, there was nothing more to do but get in the car. Georgia hurried upstairs first. She needed one last minute alone with Kaden before the finality of the memorial.

Opening the door to Kaden's room, Georgia was immediately assaulted by her memories. She could smell the faint scent of baby powder that had always surrounded Kaden. Her mind flashed to their last morning here as they dressed for the park.

Kaden had wanted to wear her purple sundress but Georgia had refused, telling her it was better to wear her shorts and tee shirt to the park. Kaden's big eyes had turned sad with her plea to Georgia to wear "her most beautiful dress." Georgia had prevailed and they had gone out for the day in shorts and the pink Hello Kitty tee shirt. Now the purple sundress lay across Kaden's bed, waiting to be hung in the closet, and Georgia wished she had let Kaden wear the dress.

She picked it up and inhaled the material deeply. A wave of sadness overcame her and she sank to her knees.

Ryan found Georgia a few minutes later, crumpled on the floor by the bed, the purple sundress clutched to her chest as she rocked her body back and forth and cried.

CHAPTER 6

GEORGIA REMEMBERED ONLY BITS AND PIECES of the memorial service. The day passed in a fog. She endured the service and was vaguely aware of Ryan and Caroline standing with her by the tiny casket, as friends and family filed past. Nothing made much of an impression on her. People told her the sermon was beautifully done; they tearfully shared memories of Kaden and offered to call in a few days. The one thing Georgia could focus on through the day was that at the end of it, she would be going home to a house Kaden no longer inhabited. The moment came and Ryan, Georgia, and Caroline drove slowly home. The drive was over much too quickly and they silently went into the house. The quiet enveloped them.

An overwhelming fatigue had descended on them and by silent consent, Caroline went straight to her room. Ryan closed the bedroom door behind him as Georgia fell across the bed. Ryan kicked off his shoes and lay down beside her. Holding her against his body, they both fell into a sleep of emotional exhaustion.

The sound of knocking woke Ryan. Startled, he looked at the bedside clock. He had slept for three hours. Pulling his arm gently from underneath Georgia, Ryan sat up. The knocking sounded again and Georgia turned restlessly in her sleep. Ryan could hear the low murmur of voices as Caroline answered the door.

Ryan quietly made his way to the adjoining bathroom and, closing the door, he splashed cold water on his face. He looked at his tired face in the mirror, visually tracing the new lines around his eyes. Then he walked quickly back through the bedroom and closed the door behind him as he headed to the entry way. He was surprised to see Caroline talking to a man he didn't recognize who was holding up a badge for her inspection.

"Okay, Detective Stanton. But can't this wait?" Caroline was asking, as she defensively held onto the door frame, refusing entry to the man outside.

Ryan cleared his throat "It's okay, Caroline. I'm here."

Caroline looked around with concern at Ryan before she opened the door wider. As the police officer stepped into the house she turned to head back to her bedroom. Ryan stopped her. "Please stay. Let's find out what's going on. Come in, Detective."

"Jack Stanton, investigating your daughter's death."

Caroline led the way into the living room and everyone took a seat. Jack Stanton had the tell-nothing expression on his face that he had spent years perfecting. His 30 year career as a police officer and now detective never prepared him fully for the things he dealt with on a daily basis. But he never showed his emotional reactions to the public. His job was to convey confidence. His strong jaw line helped. Now that his dark hair was beginning to gray at the temples and he had a couple of soft lines around his brown eyes, people usually had no problem trusting him. As Ryan went through the expected social amenities of getting everyone settled, Jack took in the well-kept house. His practiced eye noted a financially comfortable family. Nothing was too fancy that it couldn't be replaced as was appropriate for a young family. The bright sun sparkled through the living room windows. He took a seat on the beige sofa, accented with colorful pillows in blue, yellow, and green. The fireplace was obviously never used and there was only one decorative bowl on the coffee table in front of him.

"Is Mrs. Maxwell home?" he asked.

"She's resting. It's been—" Ryan hesitated a long moment before finishing "It's been a hard day."

"I understand," Jack said carefully as he took his notebook from his jacket. "I do need to talk with her soon. Were either of you present at the time of the attack?"

Ryan sat silently for a moment as the implication of this visit washed over him. Leaning forward he looked at Jack intently. "Detective, why are you here? I thought the police would file an accident report."

"Yes, normally they would. We have reason to believe something more was at play here." Jack's voice was steady as his eyes met Ryan's.

"You mean someone did this on purpose?" Caroline whispered into the silence that suddenly filled the room.

"We found the car we believe hit your daughter about three blocks away from the park," consulting his notes, Jack continued. "A beige Buick sedan was reported stolen two nights before your daughter's incident. There was damage to the car's front bumper consistent with your daughter's injury as well as remains of a broken balloon in the back seat."

Ryan took his time, trying to absorb the information. "But why? Why on earth would someone do this?"

"We also found this on the front seat of the car." Detective Stanton withdrew a plastic evidence baggie from his jacket and placed it on the table between himself and Ryan. Inside the baggie was a photograph. Ryan looked at his daughter's happy face as she smiled up at her mother, who was pointing to something out of range of the camera lens.

Detective Stanton leaned back and watched reactions as Ryan stared at the photo. Caroline had gotten up to stand behind Ryan and looked over his shoulder. She covered her gasp with her hand. "I guess that's my question, Mr. Maxwell. Why would someone do this? Do you have any ideas?"

Ryan slowly shook his head, confusion and anger battling inside him. "I don't know," he stammered. "We're just normal people. We don't have enemies."

"I think I had better get Georgia," Caroline said as she headed for the stairs. "She needs to hear this."

Ryan, still staring at the photo on the table, had no words for the detective. His mind was spinning. The idea that someone he knew could be responsible for Kaden's death was something he couldn't understand. Georgia came slowly down the stairs with Caroline right behind her.

Standing silently in the middle of the room, Georgia glanced at Ryan briefly when he got up and steered her toward the sofa. Caroline moved to a chair by the fireplace.

Jack stood and held out his hand. After a moment's hesitation, Georgia took it.

"Mrs. Maxwell, my condolences on your loss. I can't even imagine how difficult this time is for you. I appreciate your giving me a moment."

Georgia nodded to Jack but still did not speak. As she settled on the sofa beside Ryan she disengaged her hand from the police detective and folded her hands together in her lap.

"I was just telling your husband that we have some evidence to discuss." He motioned to the items on the coffee table. "It looks like someone targeted your daughter specifically. Is there any one you can think of that would want to injure you or your husband?"

"You think someone we knew did this?" Georgia's voice had a note of hysteria. "You think we know people who would do this? That we would welcome them into our lives so they could kill our daughter?"

"Mrs. Maxwell, no one ever knowingly would welcome a killer into their lives. But it does happen. I'm just trying to find the person responsible."

Jack sat back on the sofa and considered Georgia's response. She was clearly in pain and with good reason. But there was more here. There was something he didn't yet know. He kept his voice soft and low.

"Mrs. Maxwell, no one blames you. From all reports I've read, you are a caring mother. I talked to the women who were with you in the park that day. They both say you were diligent in watching out for your daughter."

Georgia's shoulders shook and she covered her face with both hands. "That's not it. I'm responsible because it's my punishment."

Ryan put his arm around her and tried to comfort her. Caroline sat forward uneasily. She cleared her throat to get Georgia's attention and gave her a warning look.

Georgia's gaze was angry then she softened and shook her head. "I'm sorry, Detective. It's been an emotional day. I don't know what I mean, really."

Jack flipped his notebook shut. "Why don't you both think about it and come down to the station tomorrow. We'll talk then." He stood up and shook hands with Georgia. "My sympathy, ma'am."

Caroline showed him the door then turned to the kitchen. Georgia floated past her on the way upstairs, silent and locked in her own world again. Ryan sat alone until twilight filled the room and Caroline called softly to tell him she had prepared dinner. With a deep sigh, he rose and joined her.

34

CHAPTER 7

GEORGIA THREW THE COVER BACK on the bed as the early morning light seeped into the bedroom. She hadn't slept much and when she did give in to her exhaustion she was troubled by her dreams. She and Kaden playing in the park, laughing, and then a sudden fear that something was wrong, something she couldn't control or change, a terror that engulfed her. Then she looked at her hands covered in red and she thought at first it was the red balloon, broken and deflated. Everything was red, it was the only color she could see. Then she realized it was blood, Kaden's blood, covering everything and her own screams woke her.

She looked around the room that belonged to Kaden. It was a happy room filled with little girl dreams. There were big butterflies painted across one bright blue wall. The toys were neatly put away in the toy chest and Kaden's dolls were lined up on their shelf, each in her own place. This was the only place Georgia found any peace of mind these days.

The last three weeks had fallen into a routine of some kind even though it still felt unnatural to her. She and Ryan had dutifully talked to the police, answering their questions and denying knowledge of anyone involved in Kaden's death. Jack continued to check in with Ryan on a regular basis, but Georgia paid little attention. Her days went by in a haze, not feeling quite real to her as she retreated further into herself.

At some point she had started sleeping in Kaden's room. Caroline had stayed for a week then gone home to San Antonio, promising to return soon. She had stayed as long as she could without her boss coming down on her. Caroline had been working at the newsroom for fifteen years, so she had plenty of seniority and lots of flexibility. But she did have a responsibility to her job and she had to get back to her own life for a while. When she left, the house seemed so quiet and neither Georgia nor Ryan could find anything to say to each other. Their conversation at first was stilted and uncomfortable and eventually, they just quit trying. They passed each other through the house without speaking, the silence slowly building a wall between them.

Ryan was trying his best to get on with life. He had his job at the marketing firm and friends there. He had his workouts at the gym. But Georgia seemed stuck. She couldn't seem to find the energy or the strength to get out of bed some mornings. She would pull the cover back over her head and pretend to sleep until Ryan left for work, then lay there staring at the ceiling, remembering. She was also starting to resent Ryan for his ability to move forward. Her conversation with Caroline haunted her nearly as much as her dreams about Kaden. The guilt she felt was eating at her, gnawing her insides, growing stronger every day. Her days passed in a blur and she couldn't remember what she did with the hours.

Every evening when he came home from work, Ryan tried to talk to Georgia. Every day it got harder to break the silence between them. Finally, Ryan resorted to picking a fight with her in a desperate attempt to elicit some kind of emotion.

Georgia sat silently as Ryan ranted on about the dirty dishes piling up in the sink and the dust gathering on the furniture.

She said nothing when he complained about another dinner consisting of warmed up casserole from their dwindling supply of frozen funeral food.

Nearly at the end of his ability to control his tirade, Ryan paced the living room as Georgia sat in a chair, staring at nothing. He stopped in front of her. "Do you even know I'm still here, Georgia? Does it even matter to you?" He waited for an answer.

Georgia slowly focused her gaze on Ryan and as she stared at him all her anger and resentment boiled out of her. "I'm not really sure Ryan. Does it matter?" she snapped. "Why are you here if nothing here suits you anymore?"

Ryan felt himself recoil slightly at the depth of rage he felt in her words. But as he met her accusing glare, Ryan felt himself fighting to keep his own anger under control. It felt good to feel something other than the all-consuming grief and despair he had lived with for the last three weeks.

"How would you know if anything suits me, Georgia? You haven't noticed anything except yourself for weeks. You aren't the only one who's suffering."

"So, it's all about you... is that it, Ryan? You seem to be doing fine with your job and your workouts at the gym. You don't have a clue how I feel."

"I'm the one person who does know, Georgia. I lost my daughter. Our daughter, you know the one you were supposed to be looking out for? The one you were supposed to protect? The one who died on your watch?" Ryan regretted the words as soon as he heard them. He knew he had gone too far.

He was about to apologize when Georgia jumped to her feet. "My daughter, Ryan. Not yours. She's my daughter." She faced him, breathing hard. Ryan's last comment had struck deep and it loosened the pain inside Georgia. Something deep inside her screamed to stop before she went too far but she pushed the voice down. It was too late anyway. She watched Ryan's face start to change as a horrible truth occurred to him.

He reached out and grabbed her arm, his fingers digging into her flesh. His voice was barely a harsh whisper.

"What did you say?"

"That's right," Georgia jerked her arm away from his grasp. "She was my daughter but she wasn't yours. You weren't Kaden's father." Georgia's moment of triumph was short lived as she watched Ryan's face turn white. He stumbled backward. One hand clutched at his heart as if he were trying to hold the pieces inside his body. His other hand reached out blindly.

"What?" he whispered again. Georgia grabbed for his arm, but he waved her away. "What?"

The word hung in the room, suspended between them. Georgia suddenly felt like there wasn't enough oxygen to breathe and she gulped for air.

"Ryan, please. Listen to me. I'm sorry. Of course, you were Kaden's father. You loved her and took care of her. You did all the things a father should do."

Ryan said nothing, staring at her. He swayed slightly, and Georgia grabbed his arm then, steering him toward the sofa, afraid he would fall before she got him seated. Obediently he fell onto the sofa and she sat next to him.

"Ryan, let me explain. Please hear me. I should have told you a long time ago. I made a mistake and I didn't know how to fix it. But then we had our baby we always wanted and life was so perfect. I didn't want to ruin it."

"Who was he? Was it a one-time fling or a long affair?" his voice was dangerously quiet now.

"No, no, it wasn't like that at all. Let me start at the beginning, okay?" Georgia took a deep breath, trying to gather her thoughts.

"We had tried for so long, Ryan, to get pregnant. All the money and the testing and all the disappointments. I wanted it so badly and I know you did too, but it was different for you. If we didn't get pregnant, you said you were okay with that and that we would be happy without kids of our own. You said we would be the kindly uncle and aunt at holidays. But that wasn't enough for me and I knew it never would be enough. I needed to have children. I wanted a baby more than anything, but it just never happened for us.

Then at work one day I got called in to Mr. Lembeck's office. It was when we worked those three weekends in a row on the Simpson/Burton case. We had also just gone through another round of hormones that failed. I was so discouraged when I got my period and I knew that I had failed again. Money was running low and I knew it wouldn't be long before we had to stop.

But Mr. Lembeck said how much he appreciated the extra hours I put in and he gave me a bonus. A big one. He said I deserved it for my years with him. I was excited. On the way home I was thinking that maybe we could take a trip and get away from all the stress. I thought it would help me get pregnant. Then I was in the car waiting at the light at Forest and Greene and I saw it right across the street. Dr. Stuart's infertility clinic. I pulled in and talked to them. They gave me brochures and answered questions about artificial insemination and I made a consultation appointment. I worried about how to tell you, but I was going to tell you, I swear. I was so preoccupied that I forgot to go to the bank, so the bonus check was still in my purse.

When you came home, I tried to talk to you but you were tired. All you wanted to do was watch the basketball playoffs. I even tried the next morning before work but when I mentioned the infertility workup and artificial insemination you laughed. You said if we couldn't have a baby the natural way, maybe we shouldn't have one. Then you left for work.

I didn't know what to do. I felt this was our only chance. I was desperate and these people seemed to have the solution. So I called in sick to work. I kept the appointment. I paid cash and I used a fake name. It was so easy that I convinced myself it was meant to be this way. They explained how they did everything and showed me around. Then they gave me donor profiles and I looked at hundreds of them. But I found a match for you, Ryan. I searched and searched until I found one that could have been you. He had the same color of eyes and hair. He was a med student so he was smart like you. His hobbies were rock climbing and soccer so he was athletic like you. I chose him because I wanted our baby to be like you."

Georgia's voice faltered as she felt Ryan flinch at her words. But she knew she had to finish now and make him understand.

"So, I chose him, a donor," she continued, her voice growing stronger as the words ran out. "I made the appointments and I cashed the bonus check so I could pay for it. I never thought about what would happen if it worked. I had the procedure done and then I waited for my period to start just like it had every month. But it didn't happen. I could hardly believe it. I waited another week then I took a pregnancy test. It was positive and it felt like it was just you and me and our baby. I kind of forgot about the donor and the procedure. I wanted to be sure, so I don't know how I did it, but I didn't say anything until I went to the doctor a week later. He examined me and confirmed the pregnancy then I came home and told you. Do you remember, Ryan? Do you remember how happy we were?"

Ryan nodded but he still hadn't looked at Georgia.

"Ryan, Kaden was your daughter. You were the one there throughout the pregnancy. You felt her first kick. You were the first one to hold her when she was born. You were there for her birthdays and skinned knees, and her first taste of ice cream. I'm so sorry, Ryan. I should have told you long ago. I should have talked to you before I did it. But we had our little girl and she was so much like you. She loved you so much." The words stopped. There was nothing more. They sat silently, side by side. Just when it seemed as if Georgia would burst if something didn't happen, Ryan raised his head. His eyes were dead. His expression scared Georgia, but she reached out for him. Ryan flinched as her fingers brushed his arm. "Ryan?"

"How could you, Georgia? How could you lie to me?" His voice was low and cold.

For a moment Georgia was stunned, thinking it would be better if he yelled or screamed at her. This Ryan scared her but she knew she could make him understand.

"Ryan, I tried to tell you. I wanted to at first. But then it just didn't matter anymore. I saw the way you were with Kaden and you were her father. In every way that mattered. And I never should have told you like this, blurting out something hurtful. I didn't mean it." Ryan stood up then sat back down. He finally got up and paced the living room, a man not at comfort with himself. He finally stopped in front of Georgia.

"So, after you've lied to me for years, I'm supposed to just believe you now? I'm supposed to just accept this? This bombshell you just dropped onto what was left of our life? Pick up the pieces again and move on? I can't even look at you right now."

He left and Georgia, thinking she had already used up all her tears, surprised herself.

CHAPTER 8

BALANCING HER COFFEE CUP IN ONE HAND with the phone tucked between ear and shoulder, Georgia pulled back the curtains again.

"He's still not home, Caroline. He was so angry. I've never seen him like that."

"Well, Georgia, he's never dealt with anything like this before. It's a lot to try to accept and understand. It will take time."

"I know, but still... he just left. I don't know where he has been or even if he's coming back."

Caroline murmured some encouragement while Georgia padded into the kitchen in her socks. When they hung up the phone, she poured out the cold coffee in her cup. Although she had been waiting for this moment, she was startled when the back door opened. Ryan's eyes were red with a lack of sleep and his scruffy, unshaved face added to the look of exhaustion.

Georgia threw her arms around Ryan, trying not to let it bother her that he didn't respond to her embrace. "Oh my God, Ryan, I was so worried. Where have you been?"

Ryan stood inside the embrace with his arms hanging at his side. He finally pulled away from Georgia and, without looking at her, started through the kitchen. His voice floated back to her. "I just need to get some things. I'm not staying."

Georgia turned toward his retreating back with a deeper sadness in her heart than she had felt in days. "What do you mean? Where are you going?"

There was no answer, so Georgia followed Ryan's path and found him in their bedroom. He was taking out underwear and socks. His gym bag was on the bed and he stuffed the items inside.

"Ryan, please, can't we talk?"

"No, we can't," he opened the closet and took out jeans and the shirts still on hangers. Laying these across the bed, he went back to the closet for shoes.

Georgia stood at the foot of the bed with her arms folded, watching. "Really, Ryan."

Holding up his hand, Ryan stopped and finally looked at her. "Just don't, Georgia." Feeling like she couldn't breathe, Georgia turned and somehow left the room. She went to her sanctuary, Kaden's bedroom, and stayed there until she heard the kitchen door close again. The silence of the empty house descended on her.

She went to their bedroom closet and, opening the door thought how strange it felt to see the empty space where his clothes had hung. With her arms wrapped around her own body, Georgia laid down on the bed, her mind as empty as her soul.

CHAPTER 9

THERE WAS NO WAY TO DETERMINE night from day. The house was shuttered, all the blinds drawn against life. Georgia slept. She spent hours in Kaden's room, touching her things, inhaling the scent of her left on her clothes. She would go to the family room and get lost in memories of her former life while looking at their photo albums. Sometimes she had trouble recognizing who the people in the photos were. They looked so happy.

She ate when she had to eat, which was less and less as the days went on. The phone rang at first but then she turned off the ringer and now the only sign of the outside world was the frantically blinking red light on the answering machine. She thought about smashing the machine just to stop the annoying reminder, but it seemed to take too much energy.

Days passed, or maybe weeks. Georgia didn't care. She felt safe in this world she had created, before all the pain. She was lying on the floor of the family room, with Kaden's stuffed panda Lulu by her side, looking at pictures of their last family vacation. They were at the beach, Kaden's first time. She loved playing in the sand, then catching waves with her daddy. In the picture, Kaden's face was turned up to Ryan, her pink nose crinkled as she laughed at one of their jokes. Ryan's arm was reaching out to go around Kaden, protecting her always, shielding her from danger, just like he did every day. Until he couldn't.

Georgia felt a sob escape her throat. He couldn't protect his daughter because she was the one in charge that day. She was the one who was supposed to protect Kaden and she had failed. Her hand reached out to the bottle of pills she carried with her now. It would be easy, she thought, to make all of this go away. She could sleep without dreaming for a while and maybe Kaden would forgive her.

Georgia became aware of a loud noise that seemed to be going on and on. Annoyed, she pulled her mind back to the present and identified the sound as knocking, loud knocking. Someone was calling her name and, as she stumbled through the house towards the front door, she saw the handle of the door turn as someone juggled it.

Numb to any feeling of fear or danger, Georgia jerked open the door to find herself face to face with two police officers.

"Mrs. Maxwell? Are you okay?" the older officer spoke first.

"Yeah, yes. What's going on?" Her voice sounded strange to her own ears as she squinted into the sunlight.

"We're doing a well check, ma'am. Your friend, Caroline Richter, reported that you have not been responsive for several days."

"Oh, I guess not." Georgia suddenly became aware of wearing old sweats and a tee shirt with no bra with her hair unwashed for weeks. Self-consciously, she folded her arms around herself and was surprised to feel her thinness. Her hand nervously brushed through her matted hair.

"I'm okay, just taking a few days to myself."

"Do you mind if we check the house for you?"

Georgia let the two officers inside, then perched on the edge of a chair as they checked each room, opening closets and looking at windows until satisfied that there was nothing amiss.

"Okay, Ma'am. You might want to call your friend, see if she can come by or something?"

Assuring them again that she was really all right, Georgia stood at the open door until the patrol car backed out of the drive and onto the street.

CHAPTER 10

BACKING OUT OF THE SAME DRIVEWAY, a few months later, she checked her mirror.

Georgia held a bottle of water in one hand and checked her watch. She knew she was running late but she didn't want to miss her meeting. She drove the four- block distance to the old church on the corner and pulled into the parking lot, waving to a couple of regulars as she gathered her keys, phone, and purse. As she got out of the car, Georgia noticed how the leaves were dropping from the trees, spreading a yellow carpet across the sidewalk.

The meeting was just starting as Georgia slipped into a chair. The door behind her closed as the facilitator's assistant put up a sign: "Grief Group in Session."

Georgia felt herself start to relax and her mind quieten as everyone introduced themselves. After six months of regular attendance, she knew most of the people here. When the police left her home that day, Georgia had looked around her house and really saw it for the first time in weeks. She looked at herself in the mirror and was shocked at the reflection of a woman beaten down. Her hair hadn't been washed in days and it was matted to her head. There were dark circles under her red-rimmed eyes. Her face was drawn and sad. She knew something had to change and the next morning she had called Caroline. Together, they found a counselor who had given her a schedule of these meetings. She had attended them nearly every day since. She missed Kaden horribly, but with help from her counselor and talking to the group members she was finding life bearable. The only thing Georgia had not been able to make better was Ryan. She called him each week. Most of the time he didn't even take the call, but she left messages for him. He was living with his friend Jace and Jace's wife, Brenda. She knew he was physically okay but he wouldn't talk to her. At night, alone in their king-sized bed, Georgia missed him, but she had stopped crying herself to sleep.

She pulled her attention back to Denise, a short brunette who had lost her 14 year-old son a year ago to cancer. The meeting came to a close after an hour and she and Denise stood by the door talking.

"Who is that guy, Georgia? Has he been here before?" Denise pointed out a slender man in his early twenties standing nearby. The counselor was giving him a phone number and the recommended reading list.

"I haven't seen him here before," Georgia replied. Just then, the man's head turned and he looked directly at Georgia, his white teeth flashing in a quick smile.

A pink flush traveled up her neck and Georgia looked at Denise sheepishly. "Oops, I got caught staring."

Denise laughed, grabbed Georgia's arm, and started toward the man. "In that case, you have to introduce yourself and acknowledge your social ineptitude. It's the only way."

The two women made their way across the room and Denise introduced herself and Georgia. The counselor patted them both on the shoulder and made a quick exit.

"My name is Joshua Lehman." His voice was deeper than expected and his handshake was quick and firm. "Do you get a lot from these meetings?"

Denise launched into a description of the group, the meetings, and her own story, giving Georgia a chance to study the newest group member. He was a handsome man, a little taller than she was and slightly built. His blonde hair was a little long and unruly. He had blue eyes and a tiny space between his two front teeth. He kept his attention on Denise, but Georgia knew he was aware of her standing silently beside him.

As Denise wrapped her story they all three strolled to the door. Then squinting into the bright sun Denise said her good-byes quickly and left the two of them on the steps to the church. Georgia smiled shyly. "Well, it was good to meet you, Joshua."

"Call me Josh, please. Do you come here a lot?"

"Nearly every day for the last six months. It's really helped me."

"Who was it? I mean, maybe, I shouldn't ask," He broke off uncomfortably.

"No, no, it's okay. I don't mind talking about her. My daughter, Kaden, was hit by a car. Six months ago."

"I'm so sorry. That must be awful."

Georgia nodded. "It is. How about you?"

"Oh, my father. I didn't know him very well but still, I guess, it's just knowing we'll never have a chance to know each other." He looked away from her then fumbled in his shirt pocket for sunglasses. "Well, I guess I better go. Maybe we can talk more sometime?"

Looking at him for a moment, Georgia hesitantly reached out and touched his arm as he turned to leave. "I don't really have anything to do now. Want to grab some lunch?"

Josh turned back with a quick smile. "I'd love that."

CHAPTER 11

THEY WENT TO A SMALL LUNCH COUNTER and had sandwiches with iced tea, ham and Swiss for Georgia and an Italian sub for Josh. He fiddled nervously with the potato chips on his plate before taking a huge bite of sandwich. He chewed solemnly but when he saw Georgia watching, grinned at her with his cheeks full. Swallowing, he took a sip of tea and laid the sandwich on his plate.

"So, Josh, tell me about yourself. Where are you from?"

"I grew up here. My family moved here when I was a kid. My dad and I were never really close. He worked a lot, I guess. I was close to my mother, but she died a few years ago. I didn't have any brothers or sisters so it's just me now. I rent a room over on Terranova."

"Terranova? Isn't that somewhere to the east of here? Not a great part of town, is it?"

"No, but the rent's cheap. I don't know many people, so I don't have company. It's not a place people want to go anyway.

57

I'll get something better when I can, but I'm just trying to get on my feet now. I work construction a little but work is kind of hit or miss."

"Have you thought about going back to school? That might help."

"Yeah, that sounds great. Maybe you could help me? Just talk me through it and stuff?"

"Sure, I would love to do that." The conversation dwindled to a comfortable silence as Georgia sipped her tea.

"Tell me about your daughter. What was she like?" The question came softly

Georgia looked at him for a minute, assessing this potential friend, and wondered how much to tell him. Something made her want to trust this man, she realized, looking at his quizzical expression and wide blue eyes. In a way, he nearly reminded her of Kaden with his innocence and openness.

"She was wonderful. Kaden was only five years old. She was bright and funny and beautiful. She had so much potential."

"How did she....you know?"

"It's okay. She died. You can say it." Georgia sipped her tea. She set the glass down carefully before she answered. "She was run down by a murderer in a car. Running for a balloon and a monster used his vehicle to kill her."

Josh sat silently while Georgia looked away for a moment, blinking away tears.

Then he cleared his throat and spoke softly. "Killed? You mean on purpose?"

Georgia lifted her head and her steady gaze met his look. "Yes, that's exactly what I mean. Someone ran over her on purpose."

"Wow, do the police know anything? Are there any leads?"

"Not yet. The car was stolen. They didn't find prints. But I'll never give up. We'll find who did it."

"Wow," Josh said again. "You just don't often hear that kind of thing happening to someone you know. I'm so sorry."

He reached out and grabbed Georgia's hand, turning her wedding ring around and around on her finger.

"How is your husband taking it?"

Surprised by the intimate gesture and gently taking her hand back, Georgia smiled sadly, "Ryan is hurting. It's hard for him."

"Well, sure, but it's hard for you, too! Is he supportive toward you? Does he come to group too?"

"No, he doesn't come." Georgia shook her head and took a deep breath to calm herself. "But, yes, he's as supportive as he can be with his own grief."

As the lie fell from her lips, Georgia justified it to herself. She liked Josh, but she wasn't going to throw her husband under that bus for him.

"Let's talk about your dad. You said you weren't close?"

Josh threw their sandwich wrappers in the trash and pulled his glass in front of him. "It's not that we weren't close exactly. I never really knew him. He kept a lot of secrets. Some stuff I just found out about after he died. I guess that's why I came to the group. I'm still trying to figure out who or what I lost."

"That can be harder than anything, I guess, losing a dream."

"Anyway, I'll be okay. I just would have liked to know him."

His voice broke. As he stopped talking, Georgia watched his face concentrating on the straw he was twisting in his hands and thought how childlike he appeared. He was just a lost little boy, looking for his dad. She reached out and patted his shoulder.

"It's okay, we all have these feelings. It helps to share them."

Josh smiled shyly as he glanced up at Georgia and nodded.

Feeling maternal towards him, Georgia left her hand on his shoulder. "I'm at the meeting nearly every day. Do you want to meet me there tomorrow?"

Josh nodded. "Yeah, that would be great. "He wiped at his eyes.

Georgia let go of him with a final encouraging pat and pushed back her chair. "Okay, let's get out of here."

They gathered their things and Josh reached around Georgia to open the door, his other hand grazing the small of her back. "Thanks, Georgia. For the time, I mean. I really appreciate it."

They went their separate directions at the street and Georgia felt a lighter spring in her step. It felt good to help another person.

CHAPTER 12

JACK STANTON TOOK A DEEP BREATH and flipped the file on his desk back to the beginning. He had already read it front to back three times this morning, hoping something new would turn up. So far nothing had. He had another two months before this case went cold and he hated that thought. This one, in particular, bothered him. Why would anyone target a child? He reached for his coffee and made a face when he sipped the cold liquid. Station house coffee was bad enough hot and fresh, it was awful cold. He pushed away from the desk and took his cup with him for a refill.

Returning to the desk, Jack blew out his exhaustion on the hot coffee and looked at the notes again. His only break had been finding that car, but he hadn't been able to find anything else. It had been stolen from a Walmart parking lot the day before the murder. The parking lot camera was broken. No one there had seen anything, and the owner admitted that she had a bad habit of leaving her car unlocked with the key under the front floor mat whenever she ran into a store for a "hot minute" as she had that day.

The pictures of the little girl found in the car were clearly a warning. She had been the target. The motivation was the puzzle. A five-year-old girl had not done something so heinous to warrant a death hit, so it had to be revenge against one of the parents. Nothing had turned up so far on either one. From interviews with friends, coworkers, and neighbors, they appeared to be a loving couple who worked hard and cared for their child. But he was missing something. Maybe it was time for another visit with the father. Jack finished the coffee in a gulp and grabbed his jacket as he headed to his car. He had a good idea of Ryan's schedule now thanks to the surveillance he had run the first months after the incident. He headed to the gym where Ryan worked out each morning before walking to work. He had been spending most of his spare time at the gym since he moved out of the family home a few months ago.

Jack circled the block twice before he saw Ryan headed toward his office, a gym bag slung over his shoulder. He pulled the car up behind him, tapping the horn gently, and leaned over to open the passenger door.

"Ryan, hop in. I'll give you a ride."

Ryan hesitated for only a second as he realized Jack's request was more of an order before climbing in the car. This was not the first time Jack had picked him up for a quick questioning that seemed to never produce any results in finding his daughter's killer. He threw his gym bag on the floor board and buckled the seat belt without a word.

Jack took a minute to work his way back into traffic then looked at Ryan who was silently waiting for him to start the conversation. "So how are you doing?"

"I'm fine. Do you have any leads in my daughter's case?"

This was the way all of their conversations started and Jack wasn't put off by Ryan's brusque manner.

"That's why I wanted to talk, Ryan. We haven't found any other evidence from the car. It was wiped clean except for a couple of smudged prints that didn't leave enough for a match. The pictures of Kaden were the same, no prints. Can you think of anyone who would hold a grudge against you or your wife?"

Ryan swiped his hand over his eyes. It was the same question Jack always asked him and it was the same question that kept him from sleeping at night. "I don't know. I don't know. Sure, there are guys who don't like me, work issues and stuff. But nothing to even come close to this." It was the same answer he gave every time he and Jack talked.

"Somebody knows something. We'll find him." Jack braked for the light and glanced at Ryan. He liked the guy. "How are things at home?" he asked as traffic surged forward with the light change.

Ryan stared straight ahead, ready for his stop. But then he shrugged knowing he had no secrets from this guy. "Things at home are nonexistent. Things at my one-bedroom apartment are fine. Have you seen Georgia? Do you know how she's doing?"

Jack pulled in front of Ryan's office building and stopped in the drive-up. "You haven't talked to her?"

Ryan shook his head. "Not really. She calls me when the bills come in and I pick them up, usually when she isn't at home."

"She's okay from what I can tell. She's going to a grief group. It seems to be helping her. Maybe you should call her."

Ryan grabbed his gym bag and the handle of the car door at the same time. "Maybe I will. Sometime. Thanks for the ride."

He was out of the car and halfway up the steps in a second.

CHAPTER 13

GEORGIA GLANCED AROUND HER as the seats in the meeting room started to fill. She was looking toward the door when she was startled by a tap on her shoulder. She saw Josh's smile as he slid past her and sat in the chair she had saved for him.

"Made it," he grinned at her.

"Just barely, Josh," Georgia playfully slapped his arm. "You cut it pretty close today."

They settled into a comfortable comradery as the meeting started. For an hour, they listened to other survivors talk about their grief, some doing well and some struggling.

After the meeting Georgia was happy to see Denise speak to Josh as he started across the room to speak to someone. Then she turned to Georgia.

"Hey, girl, glad to see you. You and Josh have been spending some time together?" Denise's curiosity was tinged with concern.

Georgia gave Denise a quick hug to reassure her. "Don't worry. It's nothing more than you did for me when I started. He's just a lost kid and it helps me fill my day."

"Still nothing from Ryan?" Denise asked.

"Every time we talk we just end up saying hurtful things to each other. Josh suggested that we should just stay away from each other for a while."

Denise's face tensed up. "Josh suggested? Are you taking relationship advice now from that 'lost kid'?"

Georgia started to laugh but one look and she knew Denise was serious. Just as she started to answer, Josh appeared at her side. "Are we ready to go? I'm starving. Here's your purse."

Georgia took her shoulder bag from Josh. "Sure, I'm ready." She leaned over to hug Denise again who was watching them carefully. "Don't worry. It's fine."

"You be careful, Georgia." Denise hugged her back then quickly walked away.

"What was that?" Josh snapped with irritation as he watched Denise walk away. "Does she have a problem with me?"

"Oh, of course not! Come on, let's go." Georgia headed for the door, certain that Josh would follow her. As they reached her car, Georgia flipped the keys to Josh. Driving seemed to put him in a better mood and she wanted to distract him from Denise's reaction. Josh grabbed the keys and got behind the wheel. As Georgia settled into the passenger seat, he sat with his hands on the wheel, looking straight ahead. Then he turned to Georgia with a laugh. "Oh well. I'll just to take extra care with Denise."

He started the car and spun out of the nearly empty lot, his good mood suddenly restored. Georgia relaxed as Josh navigated the streets. She had pushed thoughts of Ryan out of her mind after their last blow up, but now the conversation came rushing at her as she stared unseeing out of the window.

After months of not answering her calls, Ryan had finally picked up when Georgia called on a Saturday morning. At first she was so stunned to actually hear his voice that she couldn't say anything. Tears filled her eyes as she heard Ryan repeat the word *hello*.

Then, before he hung up thinking no one would answer, she stumbled her way into the conversation. She asked about his health, his job, his apartment. His answers were short and to the point. He didn't ask anything about how she was doing. Her chatter dwindled and long silences filled the airtime. Finally, when she couldn't stand it anymore, Georgia pleaded again.

"Ryan, we have to talk about it. I know you are angry and I don't blame you. But we have to find a way through this."

"Do we, Georgia? Why?" his voice was harsh, wounded.

Taking a deep breath, she plunged in. "Because I love you, Ryan. I want you to come home. Don't you want that too?"

The silence nearly broke her.

Taking a gulp of air, Georgia waited. Just as she thought Ryan must have put the phone down and walked away she heard his voice, quiet and filled with pain.

"That's the hard part, Georgia. I love you too. I thought we had something special together. But it was a lie, down to its core, it was a lie. I don't understand how you could do that. I know you're sorry. I know Kaden was my daughter in every way but one. But I just can't talk to you about it right now. You and Kaden were my life. Every time I see you or talk to you I feel like I'm losing that life all over again. Can you understand that?"

Georgia had held her breath through Ryan's speech and now a huge sob escaped as she gasped for breath. She heard Ryan one more time say, "I'm sorry" before he hung up the phone. Since that day, a month ago, she had done her best to stay busy and not think about him. Josh had helped her to do that with his easy laugh and always being ready to go to a meeting, a movie, shopping, lunch. She owed him so much. Georgia's attention came back to the present and, as her eyes focused on the passing landscape, she turned to her friend.

"Josh, we passed the diner long ago. Where are we headed?"

Josh looked over at her as he maneuvered traffic and got on the highway. "Well, welcome back. Thought I lost you for a while there."

Georgia looked down at her hands, clenched together tightly. She made them relax and forced a smile into her voice. "Well, I'm back now, and you haven't answered my question. Where are you taking us?"

"I just thought a change of scenery would be good for you. I found a great little place just up the highway. We'll be there soon."

Georgia smiled and relaxed a bit more into the car seat. It was nice to watch the town give way to countryside. It was so much more peaceful and stress-free letting Josh take over. She gave herself over to the feeling of not being in control. Closing her eyes, she felt her body go limp and knew Josh was right. A change of scenery was just what she needed.

CHAPTER 14

CAROLINE RANG THE DOORBELL for a third time, leaning hard on the buzzer. She knew no one was going to answer. She had been standing on the doorstep for at least 15 minutes already. Georgia's car was not in the drive and the house felt empty. Leaving her bag on the front step, Caroline went around to the back of the house. She knew Georgia kept a spare key hidden under the third pot of flowers from the left on the patio and she shifted the pot over as she bent down for the key. Opening the door to the house, she went through the kitchen, the dining room and on to the silent living room to the front door where she unlocked the door and gathered up her bags. After taking everything to the spare room closest to Georgia's where she always stayed, Caroline went back downstairs to the kitchen, wondering what to do next. Everything seemed to be in place, but Georgia knew she was coming in today. They had talked just a couple of nights ago when Caroline told her she was able to arrange coverage at work. They had discussed plans and Caroline would drive up from San Antonio in the afternoon. Georgia might have had to run out for something, but there was no note or message. Bypassing the Keurig on the counter, she put some water on for tea and decided she would wait a few minutes and see if Georgia showed up. Just as the tea was steeping, Caroline heard a car pull into the driveway and excited voices floated to her as car doors slammed. She picked up her tea and took it to the kitchen table and sat down.

The back door opened with a wave of energy as Georgia burst into the kitchen, closely followed by a young man with long blond hair that curled around his ears. They were laughing at something the man said as Georgia grabbed Caroline's shoulders in a big hug, kissing her cheek.

"Oh Cari, I'm so glad to see you. I'm sorry we were late. Time just got away from us and I knew you would remember where the key was and let yourself in."

Caroline patted Georgia's arm, trying to take in the barrage of words as she looked at the man who had moved confidently into the kitchen and was putting leftovers in the fridge. She felt like she was the only one who had missed out on the joke but she tried to not let her feelings show.

"It's okay. I haven't been here that long." She kept her gaze pointedly fixed on the man. "I don't think we've met before."

Josh straightened up and looked at Caroline for a minute as he assessed her. His expression was blank, but there seemed for a moment to be an air of hostility surrounding him. Then he smiled and held out his hand, but the feeling remained.

"Josh Lehman. Georgia has told me about you." The words sounded like a warning more than a welcome.

Caroline took his hand and felt his cold fingers press into her hand a little harder than necessary.

"It's nice to meet you too, Josh. I don't think Georgia has mentioned you to me. You must be new friends?"

Josh and Georgia looked at each other and burst into laughter again. He moved behind Caroline so that she had to turn in her chair to see him as he put both arms protectively around Georgia. She tilted her head onto his shoulder for an instant before replying. "Yes, you could say that. Josh and I met at my grief support group. You know I go to the one on Pine and Sycamore? He has been going nearly every day for several months now."

"Georgia has been helping me with some things, Caroline. We've gotten very close." Josh let Georgia go but stayed standing next to her.

"Yes, I see. Well, that's great. I look forward to getting to know you better myself."

Caroline let the conversation die out and the silence stretched painfully until Georgia finally looked at Josh and said, "Thanks, Josh, for a great afternoon. See you tomorrow?"

For a brief moment, Caroline wondered if Josh was going to take the hint but then he smiled and turned to the door. "Bye for now, Caroline. Georgia, will you be at the meeting tomorrow?"

"Maybe. I do want to spend some time with Caroline. I'll call you tonight."

Josh turned his back and walked out without another word, slamming the door behind him.

"Well, so that's a new development. Why haven't you mentioned him before?" Caroline let her questions linger in her words.

Georgia grabbed a mug from the cabinet and filled it with water from the teapot. "Oh good, this is still hot." She rummaged for a tea bag and then sat down at the table. "I do like tea the old-fashioned way, don't you?"

Caroline stirred her tea, waiting for an answer. Georgia clearly did not want to tell her about Josh and she wondered why. She said nothing until Georgia finally laughed and shook her head.

"Oh, come on Cari, Josh is harmless! He's just a kid trying to find his way and it helps me to help him. We go to meetings together and hang out a little. There's nothing to tell."

"Okay, Georgia. As long as you know what you are doing."

"Of course I do. We just ran late from lunch. I am sorry, okay? Josh surprised me with a drive to the country and lunch at this great little out of the way place and time just got away from us. We were just having a little fun and it felt good to relax a bit." Then, taking a sip of tea, Georgia reached out to Caroline's hand across the table and a bit more contritely added, "I really am sorry. Honestly. I should have called or something. I just didn't think."

"It's okay," Caroline gave in, not wanting to create drama that wasn't necessary. "I know things happen and it's been a while since I've seen you laugh so much. It looks good."

They sat and talked, catching up on events, until the evening twilight seeped into the room, and all was well for them. But that evening after agreeing that neither were hungry enough to go out for dinner, Caroline went to her room for a hot shower and early bed. She could hear the dim undertone of voices as Georgia phoned Josh and Caroline wondered whether it was just her own jealousy that made her not like him or if he really was as threatening as he seemed. She decided it must be her own reaction to someone else being so close to her friend. Georgia seemed to trust him and Caroline trusted Georgia. Still, as she let her clothes fall to the floor and slipped under the spray of hot water, Caroline felt her gut instinct rise up again. Something was off course here, but she had no idea why she felt this way. She couldn't put it into words, but she didn't like Josh Lehman and she certainly didn't trust him.

CHAPTER 15

THE DOOR CREAKED OPEN QUIETLY. He stepped into the gloom, the smell of urine and old food hitting him like a fist. Closing the door behind him, he stood for a minute assessing the silence. He knew she was here. She was always here, waiting for him. If he was good enough, he might get past the hallway without her seeing him. He had to try. But moving slowly, he shifted his weight to take the first step and the old house gave him away. The board beneath him groaned and he froze.

"Is that you? You no good little pissant! Did you finally come home? Get in here now!"

He shuddered at the sound of the vicious voice but squared his shoulders and stepped into the room. "Yeah, it's me. What do you want?"

He ducked just as a beer bottle came flying across the room. It whizzed by so close to his head that a fleck of foam hit his upper lip. "Jesus! What are you doing?"

"Don't you raise your voice to me. Your father would have never stood for that and you know it! Where have you been? And don't sass me."

He looked at the old woman stuffed into the couch. Her hair was stringy and hadn't been washed in a couple of weeks. Her dress was stained with food and dirty dishes were piled around her in a nest on the couch. He could feel his revulsion rise up in his throat.

"Answer me! If your father were here, you wouldn't treat me this way." The old woman's voice suddenly went from angry and harsh to whining and cajoling. "You know you're the only thing I have left in this world, Johnny boy, since your father left me with you to raise by myself with no money. It's his fault I'm like this, Johnny. It's his fault. Don't look at me that way, like you hate me. You know you're all I have, Johnny."

He stood in the doorway, listening to the same story he had been told since he could remember. Feeling the wave of shame and guilt wash over him no matter how hard he tried to push it away. If only his father hadn't left them, life would have been different. If his father could have only loved him enough to stay. If his father had stayed around, he wouldn't be stuck like this. He hated his life. He hated his mother, but he loved her too. Taking as deep a breath as he dared in the fetid air, he walked into the room. "What do you need, Mother?"

The gnarled hand clawed at him and he reached out and took it in his own.

"Can you sit a little while?" she pleaded. "Just talk to me a little while, Johnny Boy."

He cringed as her voice grated over him. Sometimes he hated this more than the viciousness, this pleading, begging tone of hers. It was always like this, back and forth, the mood swings getting worse, the temper and foul mouth getting worse. He didn't know how much longer he could take it.

He sat back on the dirty couch and let her words wash over him.

CHAPTER 16

CAROLINE SAT AT A BENCH BESIDE THE WATER, letting the peacefulness of the park lull her into a drowsy frame of mind. So much had happened, and she had thought the worst was behind them, but she might have been wrong. That's why she had encouraged Georgia to go on with her regular schedule today and get to that meeting she loved so that they had a little time apart. As soon as she could, Caroline had called Ryan and now she was waiting to meet him here.

The sun warmed her face and she closed her eyes, feeling its heat warm her skin until a shadow fell across her. Opening her eyes, she saw Ryan standing before her.

Caroline reached her hand up to him and pulled him down beside her to hug him. He was thinner than she remembered and when he pulled away from her and smiled, his face was tired and worn.

"You haven't been sleeping have you?"

"Not much, but enough to get by." Ryan handed her a cup of coffee and a cinnamon roll wrapped in a cellophane paper. "Best breakfast money can buy."

"You got it." Caroline bit into the cinnamon roll greedily and savored the sweetness in her mouth for a moment before gulping the hot coffee. "That's great."

Ryan looked out over the water, his own roll and coffee forgotten. "How is she?"

"I won't lie to you, Ryan. I don't like how things are with you two." Caroline reluctantly set aside her roll and licked her fingers clean. "Do you think there's any chance at all for you?"

"I don't know. I love her. There's so much between us now and every time we try to talk it just seems to end up as an argument."

"Do you want a divorce?" The question hung in the air as Ryan gave it thought.

"No, I don't think so."

"Okay, then at least we have a place to start, Ryan." Caroline felt renewed. She could tackle this problem, as long as she knew the objective. "Georgia is coping as best she can. I know she feels terribly guilty for what she did to you and she feels guilty for Kaden's death."

"I don't blame her for Kaden."

"I know, Ryan, but she blames herself. She needs you to help her get over that. I think that grief group she goes to has helped her a lot. But, there is one problem. She seems to have gotten close to a young man who also goes there. Joshua Lehman. Have you met him?"

Ryan shook his head.

"Okay, well, like I said, he's young. But he seems to have lots of free time and Georgia thinks she's helping him by spending so much of her own time with him. I don't think it's anything more than that for her. But there's something about this guy that I just don't like. I only met him one time but I just get a gut feeling about him and I don't trust him."

"I don't know what to do about that Caroline."

"I think if you and Georgia really talked and made a sincere effort to work past some of the hurt you've inflicted on each other, she may see things in a different light. She needs you and she needs the possibility of your life together to pull her back into trying to live that life. Do you think it's worth giving it one more try?"

Ryan put his arm along the back of the bench and held Caroline's shoulder tightly in a firm hug. "You're a good friend, Caroline, to both of us."

"Yes, I am." Caroline smiled as she picked up the rest of her cinnamon roll. "Just don't you forget it!"

CHAPTER 17

THE PHONE RANG TWO DAYS LATER. Caroline had left that morning, after spending as much time as she could with Georgia. Josh seemed always to be around and it definitely put a strain on their friendship. Georgia knew that things were different now, but she really couldn't understand Caroline's instant dislike of the boy. He could be a little overbearing at times, but he seemed harmless. Now that Caroline was gone, Georgia really missed her. Running to grab the phone, Georgia hoped it was Caroline calling to say she had gotten home safely and they could connect a bit more like they always had when nothing came between them, not even Ryan or Kaden. That was strange, Georgia thought, as she reached the phone. Ryan and Kaden hadn't put a wedge between her and Caroline but Josh had definitely created a distance between them. She didn't have time to think about it more as she breathlessly answered "hello," expecting to hear Caroline's voice at the other end.

"Georgia?" the deep resonance of Ryan's voice filled Georgia's soul and for a minute she couldn't breathe. "Are you there?" he repeated when she didn't say anything. "Yes, yes I'm here. How are you, Ryan?"

"I'm okay."

There was a different kind of silence over the phone line as they both waited for the other to speak. Finally, Ryan, feeling uncertain but determined, spoke up.

"I wondered if maybe we could talk sometime, Georgia. Just really talk. We could have coffee or dinner somewhere?"

Georgia ran her hand through her hair. She was terrified and excited. She was sad to hear the distance between them and ecstatic to think they might be able to build this bridge after all. Mostly, she was just glad to hear Ryan's voice.

"Yes," she replied quickly. "Yes, we could do that. I would like that. When?"

"Tomorrow at the Blue Orchid? 7:00?"

"That would be great."

"I'm not sure what this means, Georgia."

"No, that's okay. I mean, I don't either. Let's just have dinner and talk and we'll see, okay?"

"Okay, see you then."

Ryan hung up and Georgia held the phone receiver to her chest in both hands and stared at it. She couldn't believe it. This was the first time Ryan sounded like he just wanted to talk to her, not jab or poke at the wound Kaden's death had caused. She stood like that for several minutes, not even knowing when the back door opened and he stepped into her space.

Walking into the room without a word, Josh walked up to Georgia and took the phone from her hand. "Who are you talking to, Georgia?" He put the phone back on its cradle.

"Oh Josh, isn't it wonderful? That was Ryan and he wants to talk .We're having dinner tomorrow night!"

"Really? I thought you and I were going to see that new George Clooney movie you were so hot on."

"Oh, well, we had talked about it but this is such a great thing. We'll see the movie another time. Josh? You aren't really upset are you?"

"Yes, I am Georgia. We just get rid of Caroline and finally have some time to spend on our own and the first thing you do is take off to see Ryan. I am upset and I'm angry. You're just pushing me away, aren't you?"

"Josh! How can you even think such a thing? Of course I'm not pushing you away. Where is this all coming from? And what do you mean we 'got rid of Caroline?' She's my friend, Josh, and it's okay if you don't like her, but she's going to be around a lot."

Josh stood toe to toe with Georgia for a few minutes, glaring at her, and then he laughed. "I really had you going there didn't I?"

Georgia relaxed in a nervous giggle. "I guess you did. I thought you were serious."

"Who, me?" Josh was laughing hard now. "Right, like I would be mad over something like that?"

Georgia relaxed. For just a minute she had thought Josh was truly angry and she didn't understand why it had frightened her. She laughed and, reaching out, brushed the hair from Josh's eyes. His eyes looked hard, like his laugh didn't quite reach that far. Josh grabbed her hand and held it to his chest. He suddenly became serious again.

"Just don't push me out, Georgia. Don't ever do that to me."

"Josh, don't be silly. You are my friend, too. There's room for everybody. Come on, let's get to dinner."

She put her worries out of her mind and handed her car keys to Josh.

CHAPTER 18

THE BEDROOM WAS A SHAMBLED MESS. Dresses were thrown out of the closet, landing on the bed or the floor. There were shoes scattered across the rug by the bed. And Georgia was in her closet, frantically swiping through the clothes that hung there, trying to decide yet again if she should change clothes. Finally, she sighed and stepped in front of the mirror again. The dress she had on hugged her body and the color was good on her. The dress was a pale blush color and with her tanned skin Georgia had to admit she looked pretty good. Those workouts she had started at the gym a couple of months ago were helping too so her body felt firm and strong. Spending the afternoon at the salon for a massage and getting her hair done hadn't hurt either. What was the matter with her? This was just dinner with her husband, yet Georgia hadn't been this nervous on their first date. She finally slipped her feet into her low heels and added a pair of gold hoop earrings to complete her look. Surveying the results she had to admit it was just the right look, dressed up enough to give her confidence but casual enough to not scare Ryan to death.

Straightening her skirt one last time, Georgia grabbed her purse and went downstairs to the car. Backing out of the garage she thought again about her last conversation with Josh. He had been angry with her for some reason but had covered it quickly with a laugh and turned everything on her. She thought it was a strange reaction and knew she needed to clear the air with Josh the next time she saw him. But tonight was not the time to think of him. She cleared the driveway and headed to the Blue Orchid. She didn't notice the beat-up old car parked in the shadows half a block from the house or the man slouched in the driver's seat, waiting for her to leave.

The restaurant wasn't crowded, but it took a minute for Georgia to see Ryan sitting in a quiet corner. For a quick heartbeat she wondered if she had been stood up before he half stood at the table and motioned to her. Her breathing quickened as she followed the waiter to the table so that by the time he reached out for her hand, she was a little breathless. Ryan squeezed her hand then let go quickly and waited until the waiter had seated her before he sat back down.

Georgia put her small clutch beside her on the table and studied Ryan's face, looking for a sign of his feelings. He looked wonderful to her and she realized she was staring at him as the silence stretched between them.

Laughing, she picked up her glass of water and held it out. "Thanks, Ryan, for asking me here."

Ryan dipped his water glass in her direction and smiled. "I'm glad you're here. I ordered some wine for dinner."

"That's great. You know what I like."

"Yes, well, let's order and then we can talk okay?"

They both looked over the selections, Georgia stealing glances at Ryan over the top of the menu. When the waiter arrived with a bottle of wine and served them both, they placed their orders and sat back with an air of satisfaction to have gotten the preliminaries out of the way.

"How are you, Georgia?" there was a note of wistfulness in Ryan's voice as he started the conversation. "Are you doing okay? Everything okay with the house?"

"Yes, yes, everything's good. The electrician came the other day to fix the yard light, but its fine. Everything's good. How are you?"

"Good, good. Just working, mainly, and going to the gym. Stuff like that."

There was nothing to say and everything to say all at one time and Georgia didn't know where to start. It seemed neither did Ryan. They sat silently again. Their dinner salads arrived but neither of them picked up a fork.

"Ryan? I'm sorry for the way things were the last time we talked. I don't want to argue with you. I miss talking to you."

"I know. I'm sorry too. It seems like there are things we need to say, Georgia, but we get clouded up with all this anger. But I want you to know that I'm seeing someone..."

Georgia's heart broke into and she sat very still until Ryan continued.

"A therapist who has been really good to help me work through some of this stuff."

"Oh!" Suddenly she could breathe again. "Oh, well, that's great. I'm glad. Therapy has helped me a lot too."

"Yeah, so I still have a lot of work to do to get past some of this stuff. But you should know, Georgia, that I don't blame you for Kaden's death. I never did. I was so hurt and angry that you lied. I thought we were better than that and I was disappointed."

"Oh, Ryan, I'm the one who's sorry! I don't know why I couldn't be braver, strong enough to tell you the truth, before it was too late. I'm just so sorry. And I needed you so much but I know I kept pushing you away at first. Then after you found out, you were so angry, and I understand why." Georgia's voice broke as she struggled to keep her tears back. "But I'm not sorry that we had her, Ryan. You were a great dad. We were a great family."

Ryan reached his hand across to her and grasped her fingers. "Yes, we were. I'll never be sorry for Kaden. I love that little girl forever and I'll miss her the rest of my life."

"Do you think there's a way, Ryan, for us to be friends again? Can you forgive me?"

"I can forgive you, Georgia. I have already. I don't know where that leaves us, but it's a start, right?"

They smiled at each other across the table until their dinner arrived. Georgia's chicken piccata and Ryan's steak were both flanked by a side of fresh broccoli. When the waiter left Georgia looked at her plate and laughed. "Do you remember how much Kaden loved broccoli? I never saw a child eat that much broccoli!"

Ryan laughed as he picked up his fork. "I know. We never had to use any of those parenting tricks did we? She would beg for it and eat every bite."

One memory led to another and another and soon they were outdoing each other with stories of Kaden with her toys or at the park or eating pizza for the first time. The evening passed in a haze of shared happiness and they sat over coffee long after their meal was finished.

Finally, after the waiter made his third approach to their table, getting a little more intrusive each time, Ryan looked up and realized the restaurant was empty except for their table.

"Hey, I think we outlasted everyone. Our waiter wants to go home!"

Georgia reluctantly looked around her. "I had such a nice time, Ryan."

In the act of reaching for his wallet, Ryan stopped and looked at her. "I did too, Georgia. You know I still love you"

He summoned the waiter and provided his credit card while Georgia fumbled with her napkin, not knowing what to do or where to look. His last words had sent her heart pounding through her chest. She wanted to jump up and down and shout but instead she took a deep breath and sat quietly until the bill was settled, then allowed the waiter to pull her chair back and she walked sedately out of the restaurant with Ryan.

They reached the valet and Ryan handed over both their tickets. They stood silently waiting for their cars. When hers arrived, Georgia arranged her skirt carefully as she got behind the wheel and checked her seat adjustment. Ryan tipped the valet and closed her door, then leaning through the open window he kissed her quickly on the cheek and was gone. Georgia closed her eyes.

"I love you too, Ryan." She whispered.

CHAPTER 19

HE HAD WAITED FOR THE CAR to turn off the side street
and head into town. Then he waited a few more minutes to be
sure she didn't circle around and come back to the house for
something she had forgotten. When the street remained empty
and the house dark, he slowly got out of his car, quietly closing the door behind him. One good thing about this old bro-
ken-down heap, he thought, the light didn't come every time
you opened the door. Even if there was no one on the street he
didn't want to risk someone in the neighborhood recognizing
him. Keeping his head down with his hands in his pockets, he
walked quickly to Georgia's house and went around to the back
door. Using the key he knew she kept under the third flowerpot, he opened the door. For a moment he had worried that
after her friend had used the key it hadn't been replaced, but
good old reliable Georgia had put it right back under the pot
for him to find. He slipped into the house and moved around
with ease in the dark. He didn't want to turn on the light to

alert anyone, but instead used a small penlight aimed mostly at the floor to be sure he didn't stumble unnecessarily. He made his way through the kitchen and went upstairs to Georgia's bedroom. He had only been in this room a couple of times. He picked up a red dress lying across the chair and held it to his nose, inhaling deeply. Smiling, he laid it back exactly as he found it. He smiled even more as he glanced around the room and saw the disarray. This would be easier than he thought it would be since the room already looked trashed. He stepped over shoes left lying in the floor and made his way to the night table beside the bed. Opening it, he thought, *this must be his side of the bed* by the looks of the contents he shuffled through in the drawer. Not much of interest here. He moved to the other side of the bed and looked in Georgia's bedside table. A couple of books, some reading glasses, and a bottle with still a few pills described as a sleep aid. He opened the bottle and poured most of the pills into his hand and closed the bottle back up. Putting the pills in his jacket pocket, he closed the drawer and moved over to the chest of drawers. He pulled out sweaters and lingerie, letting his fingers linger over the soft feel of the material. He could smell the scent Georgia wore as it clung to her clothes. He put everything back as he found it, but he went through all the drawers, touching everything she owned, making it his. He did the same with all the clothes in her closet, careful to not touch any of Ryan's things still hanging there.

Finally, he made his way to the small office space where Georgia paid bills and kept her mail. He sat at the desk and rifled through the paperwork. A couple of bills were left on the console, waiting to be paid. He stuffed them into his jacket as well. He didn't bother with the computer on the desk. It was too easy to catch someone playing with that unless they were very clever, and he didn't have time to figure out passwords, although he knew they would be easy. He found a notebook that had phone numbers in it and tore out the page where Georgia had listed Caroline's name and address. He kept that too.

He prowled a little further down the hallway and saw the closed door to Kaden's bedroom. Ah, the sanctuary for the dead princess. He opened the door boldly and stepped in. He looked around at the beautiful little girl's room and his rage began to grow inside of him. It took hold of him until he couldn't keep it inside him any longer and suddenly he was upturning furniture and throwing dolls against the wall, smashing their smiling faces. He pulled the pink coverlet off the bed and trampled it under his feet. He tore the poster of fairies off the wall and tore it in half, leaving it strewn on the floor. Moving to the closet, he threw everything it contained to the floor in a heap. When his rage was spent and he stood panting in the middle of the room, he unzipped his pants and urinated over the pile of clothes. Zipping up his pants, he looked with satisfaction at the damage he'd done to the little room and laughed. Then he carefully closed the door behind him and made his way back downstairs to the kitchen. He grabbed an apple from the bowl on the kitchen counter and took a big juicy bite as he locked the kitchen door and replaced the key under the flowerpot.

CHAPTER 20

GEORGIA WOKE UP LATE and lay in bed with her eyes closed. She didn't want her dreams of the night before to leave her. She had come home and then called Caroline who was waiting for her call to retell every detail of the evening. She smiled drowsily, feeling like a silly schoolgirl with a crush. She and Caroline had talked into the early hours, first going over the evening then discussing what it might all mean. Would she and Ryan ever find their way back to each other? Would they end up just being good friends? Georgia didn't know, but she felt hopeful for the first time in months because now it felt like there were options. Stretching underneath the bedcovers, Georgia let the morning sun warm her as it fell across the bed. Finally, she couldn't stay in bed any longer and she reluctantly headed for the shower. Thirty minutes later, with the bathroom still steamy and her body dewy and glistening, Georgia headed to the kitchen for her first cup of coffee. She was surprised to see that it was already 10:30 in the morning. It was the first time since she couldn't remember that she had actually slept through the night and she felt refreshed and alive. She wanted to call Ryan this morning but she and Caroline had decided that she needed to hold off on that a bit and not come across as too desperate. She would wait a couple of days and then call him if she hadn't heard from him. But till then, she could float on this feeling of hope and possibility instead of the grief and sadness she had felt for so long.

Nursing her coffee and reading the newspaper passed the morning easily, and it was the first time Georgia skipped her grief group in the past 9 months. She wouldn't make a habit of it, but it felt good to have a little freedom. She put her coffee down and wandered outside and noticed for the first time that the flowers on the patio could use some attention. They were struggling from neglect but still managed to maintain their beautiful blooms of color. She pulled out the watering can and got to work. Watering the plants led her to doing a little weeding in the bed and it felt really good to feel the dirt beneath her fingers and see the small patch of weed free flower bed she managed to clear.

She was suddenly startled to hear a loud banging from the front of her house and at the same time the doorbell sounded over and over. Jumping to her feet, she brushed off the dirt and grass from her hands and knees and hurried through the kitchen to the front door. Josh was frantically banging on the door with his fists when she opened it.

"Josh! What on earth is wrong? Are you okay?"

"Am I okay?" His face was red, although from exertion or anger Georgia wasn't sure. He was breathing heavily. "Do I look okay? What are you doing?"

"Come in before the neighbors hear you. My goodness, calm down. Tell me what has happened."

"You weren't at the meeting, Georgia! You went out last night with that psycho you were married to and then you didn't show up like you always do. I was scared to death!"

"Josh!" Georgia was shocked by what she was hearing. "Josh, you need to calm down." She guided him to the sofa and sat beside him gently.

"Now, Josh, first of all I'm fine. Do you hear me? I'm fine. Secondly, Ryan is still the man I am married to and he's not a psycho. He's a good man that I hurt very badly and I'm trying to make things right with him. And, thirdly, why are you so upset? You really don't have a right to do this."

Josh glared at her. His entire body seemed to shake with his anger. Then he put his head in her hands and finally leaned over and put his head in her lap. Sobs shook his shoulders. "I'm sorry, Georgia. I didn't mean it. Please don't be mad. I just was worried about you."

Georgia was startled by his behavior but not knowing anything to do she smoothed his hair back around his ears and patted his back, attempting to soothe him.

"I just don't want anything to happen to you," his voice was muffled. "You're my friend and I love you."

"Look. You're my friend, too, but you and I need to take a step back here, okay? I love you as my friend, but I am married to Ryan. You do get that, right?"

"Of course, Georgia. I don't want to do anything to hurt you." He looked up at her, pleading. "Just don't leave me out, okay?"

"It's okay, Josh. Why don't we go see a movie, okay? It will get our minds off all this drama."

Going to a movie was the last thing Georgia wanted to do, but maybe it would help her, too. She didn't need to spend her days moping around waiting for the phone to ring. She ran upstairs to clean up while Josh used the downstairs bathroom to wash his face. When she came back downstairs, she was surprised to see that Josh was by the door, waiting for her with a smile on his face. He had completely gotten over his upset of a few minutes ago and playfully held the door open for her.

CHAPTER 21

THE NEXT MORNING, GEORGIA WOKE UP in a completely different frame of mind. She and Josh had ended up spending most of the day together. She hadn't been able to do any of the things she had planned to do, including thinking a lot about Ryan and their dinner. Josh had just been so needy, and she didn't want to leave him on his own, although she couldn't understand why he had been so upset. She had tried throughout the morning to be sure he understood that her life was still with Ryan, if he would let it be.

She rolled out bed, groggy and out of sorts. Stumbling through to the kitchen, she turned on the coffee maker and stood leaning against the sink while she waited for it to brew. Something just seemed off about the day and it hadn't even started. Finally, the coffee was ready and taking that first sip seemed to revive her a little. She glanced at the phone, noticing there was no blinking light to indicate a message and her mood sank a little lower. She decided to shrug off her anxiety and, after getting dressed, she decided to do something she hadn't done in a few weeks. Right after Kaden's death she spent nearly every minute of the day and most of the nights in her room, trying to memorize every scent, every color of her daughter's life. It had been a while since she had gone into the bedroom. Although she still kept Kaden's things there, she knew the day was getting closer when she would be able to sort through her belongings and clean out the room. She didn't want to leave it as a shrine to Kaden. She deserved better than that kind of grief. She walked steadily up the stairs and hesitated only a minute with her hand on the doorknob. Then, knowing she had the strength to handle seeing Kaden's room now, she pushed open the door.

She stood at the doorway in stunned silence, not able to move forward and not able to close the door on the horrible mess in front of her. Everything had been destroyed. Kaden's beautiful room was ruined. The posters had been torn to shreds and thrown on the floor. Her dolls lay in ruins, their smiling faces seeming horrific as they beamed at her from underneath the rubble. Her bed was torn apart and everything in her closet was thrown in a pile on the floor. Georgia sank to her knees in the doorway, unable to comprehend what she saw. She stayed that way for several minutes until sanity returned to her and her mind started to work again. Anger filled her being. This was the only thing she had left of Kaden and it had been destroyed. It was only as she calmed down a little that the implications hit her. Someone had been in her house. Someone had done this to hurt her, someone who knew her story. Someone she trusted.

Gasping for breath, Georgia grabbed the handle of the door and used it to pull herself slowly to her feet. She backed out of the room and slowly closed the door. She felt like she had to hold things together for Kaden's sake. If she lost it now, she might never come back. Very deliberately, she reached for the phone and called the phone number she had tried so hard to forget but that was etched into her memory.

He picked up on the second ring. "Detective Stanton."

"Detective, this is Georgia Maxwell. I need to report a break-in at my home. It's related to my daughter's murder."

Saying those words out loud strengthened Georgia's resolve and her voice grew stronger. "I'm at my house now. I think you need to get here. Someone ransacked my daughter's room."

"Get out of the house, Mrs. Maxwell. Don't touch anything. I'll be right there."

Georgia hung up the phone carefully, then walked out the front door. She felt there was no one in the house, but she did what she had been told to do. She sat in her car in the driveway as she waited, and she called Ryan's phone. There was no answer but her message was much the same as she had told Detective Stanton. Then she hung up and waited.

It really didn't take more than 20 minutes for the first car to arrive. It was Ryan. He hadn't called back but instead came directly to her. Georgia stood and faced him. He walked slowly over to her car then put his arms around her gently and held her shoulders as she leaned into him. It was then that Detective Stanton arrived with a patrol car. The officers entered the house with their guns drawn. Georgia could hear the sound of doors opening at first and then nothing until an officer came to get her. He escorted Georgia and Ryan into their own home where Detective Stanton was waiting for them. He motioned for them to join him and all three went up the stairs to Kaden's room.

"Mr. Maxwell, you haven't been here?"

Ryan shook his head. "Okay, it's a little alarming to see it, but let's step in."

He went ahead of Ryan and Georgia, stepping aside to make room for them to stand silently and survey the damage. "We'll get a crew in here in a minute to look for evidence. Did you notice anything missing?"

Georgia had already thought about this while waiting for the police to arrive. "No, the house looked fine. It's just Kaden's room. I haven't been in it for 3 or 4 days then today I just wanted to check it. I found it like this but I don't know when it was done."

"Okay, let's go on back downstairs and let these guys get to work." Jack motioned to the team who were waiting behind them to enter the room.

Downstairs Georgia went over her story again in detail of how she had spent the last couple of days but as she expected, nothing seemed unusual. Ryan stood silently by as she talked. Jack took notes, asking an occasional question. Finally she was finished and everyone breathed a little deeper.

The police finished their collecting and Jack gathered his notebook and jacket and with a final nod in their direction, left Georgia and Ryan alone.

"Well," Georgia motioned Ryan toward the kitchen. "Would you like something to drink?"

"Georgia, I think I should move back in to the house."

She hesitated a moment as she reached for the tea cups but then she turned to face Ryan. "Look, I want you back here. But I'm okay. Really. Don't feel like you have to move back to protect me."

"No, that's not it. I mean, of course, I want to protect you. But it's time, Georgia. We aren't back yet but don't you think we made a start the other night? And we'll work through this stuff better together than alone. Look, I'll move into the guest room, but I think it's best if I'm here."

"Okay, Ryan. I agree and I'm glad. We still need to take things slowly, but yes, I think you should move back in."

Georgia turned back to preparing the tea and they sat together at the kitchen table, drinking tea.

CHAPTER 22

GEORGIA WAS UP EARLY THE NEXT MORNING. She had a million things to do but she did want to be sure she stopped in at her meeting. After all these months of sadness and grief it would be nice to share some good news with everyone. She gathered up laundry and got that started while she straightened and cleaned the house. A couple of hours of good steady work and she just had time to put fresh sheets on the bed in the guest room before she hurried off to her meeting. Before she left she put a note on the refrigerator in case Ryan came by early with his things. Humming under her breath, she drove to the meeting room and smiled at everyone who came through the door.

As the meeting started, Josh slipped in, nearly late again as usual. Denise was already sitting next to Georgia so Josh sat near the door in the back of the room. Georgia raised her hand as soon as the meeting started. She told the group about the break-in at her house in general terms. She didn't want to share too much about that anyway but the focus of her story was the good news that Ryan was coming home.

As she told her story, Denise gripped her hand for support and after the meeting she was the first to hug Georgia. "I'm so happy for you. You guys might really work this out!"

Georgia was so excited about her news and talking to her friends about it that she didn't even notice Josh, standing by the door. He glared at her and when she finally looked at him and smiled Josh only continued staring. Georgia shrugged it off. She didn't want anything to upset her happiness today.

By the time she was ready to leave the meeting, there were only a couple of people still standing outside. Josh seemed to be gone. It was unusual for him to not even speak to her, but again, Georgia was too busy planning her last-minute shopping list to notice.

She stopped by the grocery store on the way home and picked up some fresh green beans and a couple of nice steaks. It wouldn't hurt to celebrate a little this evening when she and Ryan had their first dinner together in their home in months. It felt like a new beginning for the two of them. Kaden would always be a part of their lives and the hole she left would never be filled. But Georgia knew it was time to let Kaden go and move ahead with her life. And she knew that she wanted that life to be with Ryan.

CHAPTER 23

HIS RAGE CONSUMED HIM. It was more than he could keep inside. It took all the strength he could find to just get himself home. He had ridden his old bicycle to that godforsaken meeting and speeding home on it he couldn't wait to get away. All those stupid people with their backslapping, high-five lifestyle congratulating Georgia while all his planning fell apart. Everything he had done for the past year, everything he had put up with, and now it was for nothing.

He had worked so hard to make his point. He had given so much just to show them how bad life could be when you didn't have everything handed to you. He had planned so carefully for it all and now it was falling apart around him.

The hard part had been listening to all the whining and moaning from those horrible meetings. None of those people knew what hardship was like. They didn't know how it felt to drag your father into the house, time after time, drunk and not able to even stand up and listen to him tell you over and over again how you were never enough for him. They didn't know how it felt to have your father leave you just because he didn't want to be there anymore. They didn't know how it felt to cry and beg him to stay and watch him pull away from your hand clutching on to his pants leg. They didn't know what it did to the mind of a son to take his father back into his life, time after time, always hoping it would be different but knowing deep in your gut that nothing had changed. Then, one night after a drunken brawl that ended with a bloody nose and black eye, the most hurtful thing of all. Josh listened, his eyes tearing from the punch as he held a dirty rag to his nose, as his father told him all about a beautiful little girl he had fathered who was living a fairy tale life just a few blocks from their run-down shack. A little girl who had everything money could buy and two loving parents to buy it for her but who had been created from the very same seed that gave you your own worthless life.

Josh knew even before his father voiced the words that he would never measure up to his father's "daughter." Finally, his father had told him the truth about something. He would always be only second best. His father loved that little girl more than he ever would love Josh even though he'd never even met her.

By the time his father really did leave them for good, Josh had been told the story a hundred times. He knew how his father had fallen on hard times and to make some extra cash for his weekend partying, he would sell his blood or when his blood was too toxified, his sperm. The clinic he donated to was not very particular about where they got the donation. They had books and books outlining backgrounds for their donors, listing all their accomplishments. Most of those were made up just to sell better to potential parents. No parent wants a kid whose sperm donor is a drunk living on the streets. They all want one who plays the violin and studies astrophysics on the weekends. Josh's father had the genetic good looks, so that part of his history was true, but not much else listed on his profile was accurate. Security was lax at the clinic, so even though he wasn't supposed to do it, his father had paid off one of the employees to tell him when his sperm donation was chosen. His ego was intense and he wanted to see what kind of woman wanted him. So, he was there the day Georgia came to the clinic for her insemination. She was a nervous woman but determined, trim, good-looking. His father was so impressed that this woman had chosen him that he followed her home and through the years he watched them. It became kind of a game for him to imagine he belonged in that family. He even took Josh there one day, to try to catch a glimpse of the life that should have been his. It was only after his father was gone that Josh had gone back to the house on the tree-lined street and waited to see Georgia and Kaden.

He had gone back to his own ramshackle house with the paint peeling off the outside walls and the weeds serving as a lawn. It just wasn't fair. It wasn't right. He didn't deserve what he had gotten in life; a drunken egomaniac for a father and a whining self-centered hag for a mother.

Whenever his mother's voice would become too much to take, Josh would go the neighborhood where Kaden lived, hoping that somehow he would fit in. Someone would see him and know that he belonged there, too. But it never happened and he would have to eventually go back to his mother, sitting in the same spot she was sitting in now.

He looked at her now, her fat chin dropping onto her chest. There was a half-eaten sandwich on a paper beside her and an empty beer can fell from her hand as Josh stood there. The rage inside of him built up again, against his life and the people who had forced him to live this life. He approached his mother cautiously even though she had passed out. He picked up a pillow from the couch and, kneeling beside her, he pressed the pillow against her nose and mouth. Her eyes popped open, confused, questioning, and not able to focus on him and she feebly hit at him with her hands. But he was too strong and she was too drunk to fight him off. She only struggled for a few minutes before Josh could feel her body go limp under the pressure he exerted. He kept the pillow in place for a few more minutes then tossed it back onto the sofa and casually walked back to his room.

At least he would never again have to hear her crying out for her "Johnny Boy." He felt good as he washed his hands in the bathroom. Then he crossed the hall back to his room and fell asleep lying across the bed in all his clothes.

CHAPTER 24

DAWN WAS BARELY BEGINNING TO LIGHT the sky when Josh woke. He had slept well and felt more refreshed than he had in weeks. He had a lot to do today but he had a plan of action and it was best to get started early.

He knew this neighborhood and no one would be about much before 10:00 so he had enough time to do what he needed to do. First things first, though, so after emptying his bladder, Josh rummaged in his closet until he found the tools he needed. He went through the living room to the front door. He didn't even glance over at his mother's body stiffening on the couch, not because it bothered him, but because she was no longer significant to him. Pulling on the gloves, he closed and locked the front door behind him. Then he squatted down in front of the door and, using the screwdriver he had taken from the closet, he jimmied the door. The lock was old and it was an easy job. He made sure to jam the screwdriver into the wood of the door frame a couple of times to make it look good, then he opened the door and went back into the house. It didn't take much to clutter the house enough to make it look like an attempted burglary. He busted the television screen for good measure and opened a few drawers in the kitchen. Then, he went back to his room where he pulled out an old duffle bag and stuffed the gloves and screwdriver into the bottom of the bag. He covered them with a few clothes and his extra sneakers.

In the kitchen, he found a scrap of paper and scribbled out a note which he left on the refrigerator. Then, looking around carefully one last time, he made sure he had covered everything. Satisfied, he grabbed the duffle and went out the back door. Circling around the block he saw no one and saw no telltale twitch of a curtain for anyone looking out on the street. By the time daylight hit the street, he was out of the neighborhood and on his way. He wondered where he might find breakfast. He was famished.

CHAPTER 25

THE SAME MORNING DAYLIGHT FOUND its way into the kitchen of Georgia's house and Ryan sat at the table, reading the paper. He tried not to make any noise. It had startled him a little to realize that he no longer knew Georgia's routines and he didn't want to wake her.

A few minutes later he was more startled when the back door opened and Georgia came in, breathing a little heavy from her early morning run. She grinned at him as she refilled her water bottle at the sink.

"Hey, this is a surprise. When did you become an early riser?" Ryan was pleased that his voice hit the right note of friendliness.

"I know, who would have believed it, right? But about six months ago, when I had been up all night again, I decided to go for a walk at daybreak. It was so nice to be out at that time of day before all the hustle got started that I did it again the next day and the next. Then I just started running instead of walking and now I almost feel like I have to get out at least a few times every week. Keeps me sane!"

"Good for you, Georgia! But you need to be careful. Someone broke into the house. I mean, that's why I moved back here—to keep you safe."

Ryan broke off as what he said hit him. His face reddened and he stammered "I don't mean that's the only reason, exactly."

Georgia smiled at him. "That's okay. I appreciate you being here, but I'm not going to live in fear any more. I'm going to grab a shower. Help yourself to whatever you want for breakfast, okay?"

She was gone. Ryan sat and stared after her before he shook his head. Something had changed in Georgia since he last had breakfast at this table. He hoped it was change for the good. He got up and rummaged in the cabinet for cereal and a bowl then got the milk and had breakfast, listening to the sound of the water running in the bathroom, hoping there would some hot water left for him.

CHAPTER 26

LIFE BECAME VERY BUSY FOR GEORGIA and, before she knew it, she realized that she hadn't been to one of her grief support meetings in a week. It was funny how much she used to rely on those meetings to get her through a day now she felt like she was finally living again. She called Denise and made plans to have lunch with her after tomorrow's meeting because she wanted to see Denise and she knew the planned lunch would motivate her to go.

She had a ton of errands today and was about to grab her keys from the hook by the back door when the doorbell rang. Ryan had left early that morning for a trip to the gym before work. Georgia grimaced but putting her bag down on the kitchen counter, she hurried through to the front door.

"Josh! Oh my goodness, come in. I'm so glad to see you." Georgia had been meaning to reach out to Josh but now that Ryan was home in the evening she just hadn't made the time. Now she felt guilty for neglecting her friend for so long. Josh didn't greet her but he did step inside the house and then stood there silently accusing Georgia of not being a good friend. Georgia closed the door and taking his arm she steered Josh into the house to the living room and nearly pushed him into a chair. "It's so good to see you! I know I should have called you and there's no excuse. Time just got away from me and I feel like a terrible friend. Can you forgive me?"

Josh sat for several seconds just staring at Georgia until she started to feel a bit uncomfortable. "Hey, is everything okay?" her voice was uncertain and wavered slightly.

"I'm fine, Georgia. I haven't heard from you in so long that I wanted to check on you."

She heard the accusing tone in his voice and knew her job would be a little more difficult than she had first thought. A little irritation ran through her mind at his immature behavior, even as she prepared to placate him.

"Josh, I know I haven't been around a lot lately. It's just that with the break in and Ryan moving back here, things have changed for me. I just needed a little time to adjust, okay? Now, come on, tell me everything. What's been going with you?"

"I lost my room."

"What? What happened? Where are you living?"

"I spent the night on the street a couple of times but then I hooked up with a buddy and I'm sleeping on his couch a few days. I'll get my own place again soon."

"But what happened?"

"One of the other tenants started a fire. I lost everything. I barely made it out alive myself."

"Oh, Josh," Georgia moved to sit beside him and held his hand. "I'm so sorry. Can I do anything?"

"You can be my friend again, Georgia! I lost everything, and I felt like I lost you, too. I can't take that." Josh started to cry and Georgia patted his back. He leaned into her, resting his head on her shoulder. "You just deserted me."

"Josh, of course, I didn't desert you. I just didn't know, okay? I wasn't paying attention and that's a terrible thing in a friend. I'm sorry. Forgive me? Please?"

Josh sniffed a couple of times and then nodded his head. "I forgive you." He whispered.

"Okay, then let's move on. Do you have what you need? Can I do anything for you?"

"I'm okay. I just needed to see you but I didn't feel welcome to come here anymore, now that you have Ryan again."

"I don't have Ryan, okay? He moved back to make me feel safe and that's it. We are still a long way from being back together." Georgia had her arm around Josh's shoulder. She rubbed his back and patted his shoulder. "And even if we were, I still have time for my friends."

"Okay, it's just that I know your friend Caroline doesn't like me and I'm afraid she's going to make you change your mind and not want to be my friend. Now with Ryan back, why do you even need me around?"

"Oh, friendship doesn't work that way! And why on earth do you think Caroline doesn't like you?"

Josh sat up and pushed away from her. "I can just tell, all right? I can tell by the way she looks at me and her tone of voice. She wants me out of your life."

Georgia laughed and rose to her feet easily. "I think you are feeling just a little sorry for yourself, whether she likes you or not, and I'm not agreeing with you that she doesn't, you are my friend, and no one tells me who to like. Got it?"

Georgia went into the kitchen leaving Josh on the sofa. She came back with a glass of water and offered it to him. "You know, I have a great idea, I think you just need to get to know Caroline and Ryan and you'll see that they don't dislike you. Why don't we all have dinner here tomorrow? Caroline's coming into town and she'll be here anyway so it's a good time to get together. Come on over around 6:30 and we'll have a nice dinner and get to know everybody, okay?"

Josh pretended to consider this for a minute, staring down at the floor. Then he stood and hugged Georgia, spilling a little water from his glass down her shirt. "Okay, if you want me here I'll come for dinner."

"Great! Now I was just on my way to run some errands. Do you want to come with me or can I give you a ride somewhere?"

"No, I'm going to walk to the bus stop. I can use the fresh air to clear my head."

"Okay, if you're sure? Then we'll see you tomorrow at 6:30, okay? Casual and easy, just dinner with new friends."

Josh hugged her again, a new look of hope on his face.

CHAPTER 27

CAROLINE WRINKLED HER NOSE at the bitter taste of the coffee and put the cup down carefully on the desk. Detective Stanton finished up the report he had been typing on his computer and shuffled a few papers on his desk before he finally pushed back in his chair and surveyed the woman waiting patiently for him.

"How's the coffee?" he asked innocently, knowing the answer.

"It's a little bitter, about what I expected." Caroline was not one to back down from a challenge and she met Jack's gaze directly.

Jack smirked a little and sat forward. He liked this one. She was a no-nonsense, good-looking woman with her wits about her. "Okay, let's get to it. You have something for me on the Maxwell case?"

Caroline took a deep breath before starting to talk. She felt a little guilty going behind Georgia's back like this, but she had to be sure she had covered all the bases. Something didn't feel right about Georgia's friend Josh, and Caroline would never forgive herself if she didn't check it out. Then, when everything turned out okay, she would be able to laugh at herself and move on.

"I wanted to see if you had any ideas about this friend of Georgia's. His name is Josh and he has been spending a lot of time with her. I just don't trust the guy. There's something that seems a little off about him that Georgia just doesn't sense. He showed up very conveniently right when Georgia was very vulnerable. He's really controlling. I know it's silly but I thought you might help put my mind at ease."

Hearing the words herself, Caroline cringed inside. It sounded like a ridiculous story even to her. She had no proof there was anything wrong with the guy, nothing but this silly feeling. Sitting there, Caroline watched Jack's reaction closely for signs of irritation, but she found none. He, at least, wasn't laughing at her. He seemed to be considering her concerns as he thumped his pencil on the desk.

"Have you seen anything that makes you think he's involved in the child's death in some way?"

"No, that's just it. I don't have proof of anything. I just have a gut feeling that he's not what he seems. I know that sounds crazy."

"I've gotten a long way in this business by trusting my gut. Sometimes it's all you have to steer you the right direction."

"Georgia and I met my senior year of high school. My mom died that year before school started, breast cancer. It was

124

horrible. Dad had taken off years before so I didn't know what I was going to do. One of the school counselors stepped in and offered me a room to live in so that I could finish school. But I don't think I would have made it without Georgia. Her family moved to Granger that year and she didn't know anyone. We were kind of drawn together, taking some of the same classes. But we shared everything, clothes, secrets, boyfriends even."

She laughed a little and looked up at Jack for his reaction. He sat with a half-smile on his lips and motioned for her to continue. "We decided to go to the same college and room together. There was never anyone serious until Ryan Maxwell came along. Georgia met him during our freshman year of college. When Georgia saw Ryan, it was like her whole being focused on him. He was the only guy she ever looked at after that and he seemed just as crazy about her. So Ryan joined our little group and it's a good thing he was such a sweet guy because I could see that I was going to have to make him my friend, too. It was easy. He was funny and smart and he adored Georgia."

"What about you? Didn't you have any boyfriends?" Jack grimaced a bit as he heard himself ask the question but found that he really wanted to know.

"Oh, sure, there were a few. I never found anything like what Ryan and Georgia have, though. I tried. I even married one of them. But after a couple of years, we both knew we were just pretending something was there when it wasn't. He's a nice guy. I hear he remarried and he and his wife are expecting a baby soon."

"Does that bother you? Did you want kids?" Again, Jack found it hard that he was asking these questions but he really wanted to know the answers. He tried to tell himself that it was just his detective instincts to get all the facts of the story, but he knew there was more to it. He liked this woman and he wanted to know her.

Caroline brushed her hair back from her face. Jack liked the way she did that too, tucking her hair up.

"No, it doesn't bother me. I'm glad he's happy. I never really wanted kids myself. That's one thing that was different for me and Georgia. All her life, Georgia wanted to be a mom. It was so hard for her when they couldn't get pregnant."

Jack made a sound of surprise.

"Kaden's their child. They just had a hard time getting pregnant." Caroline shifted uncomfortably. It occurred to her that she should tell the detective the true circumstances of Kaden's conception, but it wasn't her story to tell. She made a mental note though to encourage Georgia to tell Jack the whole story before she continued.

"Georgia was so thrilled to be pregnant and Ryan couldn't have been any happier. They were a beautiful family. There has never been a little girl more wanted and loved than Kaden Maxwell. They both doted on her and spoiled her but Kaden was such a sweet little girl. They had the perfect life."

"Until now." Jack prodded gently.

"Yes, until now. I really hoped Georgia and Ryan would be able to pull together through this and maybe they would have if it weren't for Josh. I know they had a lot of issues to work through, but Georgia has changed since meeting him.

I don't know where this guy comes from really, he just showed up one day and Georgia kind of adopted him. But suddenly he's a major part of her life and right now Georgia is very vulnerable."

"I know you care about your friend and I understand your concerns. But really, without anything to go on, we don't have much of a case against this guy." Jack hated to be truthful with Caroline when he saw the fear in her eyes. "If you can bring me anything concrete, any evidence, I'll be happy to dig into him a little and see what comes up."

It was really more than she would have expected, and Caroline knew it. She picked up her purse and stood. "I'm going to Georgia's house now and we are all having dinner tonight. Maybe I'll find something when I see him tonight."

"Don't snoop around. I don't want you to do anything dangerous to yourself or that would spook him. Just try to act naturally and be yourself, okay?"

"I will. I'll be in touch." Caroline reached out to shake hands and felt Jack's strong fingers grasp hers. "I don't even know why I came to see you. I don't have anything other than a gut feeling about this guy. But I do feel better. Thank you for listening to me."

"We really are doing what we can for the Maxwells. I won't forget this case." He held her eyes a little longer than necessary in his sincerity. Caroline nodded and wondered about Detective Jack Stanton all the way back to her car.

CHAPTER 28

THAT EVENING CAROLINE SAT BACK and watched Josh at Georgia's dinner party. He was quite the performer, she thought. He seemed like the perfect guest, but every now and then she would catch him looking at Georgia when he thought no one was looking his way and, in those moments, a different man emerged. He looked calculating and unreachable, almost cruel. He watched Georgia all the time, even when she moved away from the table. He kept his head tilted slightly in her direction and kept her in his line of vision all evening long. He seemed to use any opportunity he could find to call attention to himself. He reveled in getting Georgia all to himself.

Ryan was just as unaware as Georgia. He seemed oblivious to anything out of place and played the host perfectly.

"So, Josh, do you like football?"

"Of course. I follow the game." Josh's voice was disinterested and almost rude.

Ryan continued to ask questions and tried to engage him, but Josh seemed bored and annoyed by the effort.

The conversation was stilted, and Ryan carried most of it by himself. Josh added only small bits of conversation and turned to Georgia as quickly as possible.

"Do you remember that day we saw the guy at the mall watching the game on all the TVs in the store? That was hilarious, following all the games at once." Josh laughed and put his arm around the back of Georgia's chair, protectively. Once more, he had Georgia's attention focused on him.

Caroline finally decided to test her theory and, after dinner, she made a point of shooing the men out of the kitchen, under the age-old thinking that she and Georgia would clean up the dishes. While Georgia washed the pots and kept up a steady stream of conversation, Carolyn cleared the table and made sure she picked up the glasses and plates from Josh's dinner. Using a napkin, she carefully picked up his fork and wrapped it, putting it in a drawer under the placemats. It was a spontaneous gesture and she felt foolish doing it, but it also made her feel better. In just a few minutes Josh was back in the kitchen asking Georgia if she remembered the name of a woman, a new member, who had attended their last grief support meeting. Caroline finished up putting the food in the fridge and put her arm around Georgia's waist, pulling her close in a sisterly hug.

Anger flared in Josh's face as he watched the two women. He grabbed for Georgia's arm and twisted her back around to face him, breaking Caroline's hold on her. "I wasn't through talking to you!" His jaw was clenched and he spat out the words. "Don't turn your back on me."

Georgia's mouth opened in surprise and pain at his grip on her. She pulled herself away from Josh, rubbing her arm, certain that it would be bruised by morning. "Joshua! Don't speak to me like that and don't ever manhandle me again."

The two stood face to face, glaring at each other. Behind her, Georgia could hear Ryan approach the doorway.

"What's going on here?" he demanded, softly but firmly.

"Nothing, Ryan. I've got it." Georgia answered calmly. "I think it's time we all said goodnight. Thanks so much, Josh, for coming over."

Josh glared at the three of them all lined up against him. He took a deep breath in an effort to calm himself down. He looked down at the floor for a second, then raised his head and put on his most charming smile. "Thank you so much. The dinner was delicious and the company was great. I learned a lot tonight about friends. I appreciate the lesson."

He was out the door in a minute, letting it close softly behind him, leaving the room filled with tension.

"Wow," Caroline gave a shaky laugh. "I have to tell you, Georgia that was a little scary."

Ryan moved to the door and locked it. "I know this kid is your friend, Georgia, but are you sure he's okay?"

"I never thought of him as a problem, until tonight." Georgia admitted. "I don't know what got into him, but I agree that I didn't like that behavior at all. Let's just calm down and salvage what we can of the evening and forget about it tonight."

They moved in agreement back to the living room and after a few minutes, the conversation turned to everyday events and the stress of the evening was forgotten.

Josh sat for a long time outside the house, thinking about his mistakes. He had overplayed his hand tonight and he had underestimated Caroline. He had seen her watching him and then she had actually challenged him. He would have to do something about her, but first damage control with Georgia was necessary. He needed to re-establish himself as the one in need. Georgia thought she was getting her family back, but he was still the one in control. He wasn't finished making her suffer for what she had taken from him.

CHAPTER 29

THE SKIES THE NEXT MORNING were gloomy and dark, matching Caroline's mood for once. She usually didn't get depressed, but today she couldn't seem to shake the feeling that something was not right. She felt silly as she dressed in comfortable slacks and a new top, but when she realized she was fussing with her hair for the third time, she threw down her brush in frustration. She hated to admit it to herself, but she did feel a strong attraction to Detective Stanton and since she was on her way to see him this morning, she couldn't deny that the butterflies in her stomach were caused by him. The conflicting range of emotion was a new experience for her and not one she necessarily enjoyed. She drove to the police station and used her time in the car to give herself a stern lecture on how it was natural to find a man attractive but that shouldn't get in the way of her mission. Her mission was to save her best friend because there was something off about Josh Lehman and even if she couldn't put her finger on exactly what was wrong about him, she wasn't going to stop until she had done everything she could to find out what was going on. She felt better the more she concentrated on him and the less she thought about herself, so by the time she reached the police station, she felt more confident and sure of herself.

Striding from the elevator into the police station, she held her head high and looked around. Her gaze zeroed in on Jack immediately as he stood by a file cabinet in the back of the room. She felt a little thrill when he seemed to be aware of her presence and jerked his head up in her direction. Their eyes met and then he smiled briefly and motioned to her to join him at his desk.

Squelching down her schoolgirl reaction, Caroline reminded herself again that she had a reason to be here and met Jack, reaching out her hand to shake his.

His grip seemed to linger a little and she found herself liking the feel of his hand on hers. She would have liked to keep her hand in his but she reluctantly let go. She had to remember her mission.

"Ms. Richter, nice to see you again. Please have a seat." Jack's voice was warm and welcoming. "How have you been?"

He surprised himself by asking a personal question of a client and busied himself with shuffling papers on his desk as they both sat down. He looked across the desk at Caroline's auburn hair pulled back into a messy bun and thought she looked great. Then he gave himself a mental shake and cleared his throat. He felt like a teenager on his first date. He needed to get back in control of this interview.

"I mean, how can I help you today?"

Caroline sat primly on the edge of her chair and then reached into her purse and pulled out a baggie with a fork in it, placing it on the desk.

"I feel rather foolish. This is a little CSI of me. I took this from dinner the other night with Josh Lehman. I thought maybe it could tell us something?"

She felt her face flush in embarrassment as the silence deepened and found she wasn't able to meet Jack's gaze. But he leaned forward and picked up the baggie and studied the fork inside. "Did you touch it?" he asked.

"No, I used a napkin to pick up the handle."

"When did you do this?"

"Last night, at Georgia's."

Jack picked up his phone and made a call, speaking quietly into the receiver for a moment then turned his attention back to Caroline as she continued. "Look I know this is silly. I know how ridiculous it seems. But I thought if I could just know Josh is okay as a person then I could relax a little. There is something about him that bothers me. Last night at dinner he got really angry and he grabbed Georgia and it felt very threatening to me."

"Did he hurt her?"

"No, but Georgia made him leave early. He was so angry and then he just got cold, nearly calculating. It just gives me a bad feeling."

She broke off as a lab tech came up to the desk and Jack handed her the baggie. "Thanks, Maggie. See what you come up with and let me know, okay?"

The tech smiled at Jack, nodded quickly at Caroline, and logged the baggie into her portable log book before she left with it. Caroline took a deep breath. "Do you agree with me then, Detective? Do you think something is off?"

"I don't know, Ms. Richter. But what I do know is that you are an intelligent, thinking woman and if this is raising red flags for you it's worth checking out. We'll have results on DNA in a few days and we'll see."

"Thank you. I'm sure it won't amount to anything but I'll just feel so much better."

Caroline lingered a moment and then stood up with her purse clutched tightly in both hands. Today seemed to be a day for taking risks , she thought, so she might as well take another one. "It's been a long day already. I could use a cup of coffee. This stuff around here isn't the best but I know a place just down the street that sells coffee and the best chocolate chip muffins known to man. Would you like to join me for coffee?"

CHAPTER 30

THE DAYS SEEMED TO TAKE ON A PATTERN after the dinner party that felt very comfortable to Georgia. She liked having Ryan back home. She liked coming home after a run to find him sitting at the kitchen table reading the paper or fiddling with the leaky faucet in the downstairs bathroom again. They seemed relaxed with each other and she thought it was because expectations were so low on both sides. They each had their own interests and kept busy with their lives during the day. Sometimes he cooked dinner for them, sometimes she did and sometimes they ate on their own. She was no longer relying on Ryan to make her feel better or to fix her grief. Things felt calmer between them and in the evening if they had talked or watched a television program together she felt a deep contentment, even more than she had when they were first married.

They talked about Kaden nearly every day, but it was nice now to remember her goofy grin and how much she loved to dance around the room. It made her feel alive for them again and Georgia knew she had found a way to keep her daughter with her forever. She would miss Kaden every day of her life, but she knew now that she had to learn to live without her. The pain had dulled enough so that she thought she could really do that and she knew Ryan would always be a part of that for her.

She had not gone to a grief session since the dinner party three weeks ago and today felt like a good day to go. She didn't seem to relate to the members in the same way she used to when Kaden's loss was a gaping hole in her life, but she was forever grateful for the help she had received with the group. She wanted to honor that, and she knew she could help others who were just beginning their own journeys.

She put on her favorite blue sweater and pulled on her jeans, slipping her feet into her sneakers as she grabbed her bag. She could stop by the gym after the meeting and get a workout before heading home. She needed to work out as much as she could now since she had started sending out resumes last week and hoped that she would be working again soon.

Driving to the meeting rooms, her thoughts drifted to Josh. It was strange that she hadn't heard from him or seen him since she had asked him to leave. She had tried to call his cell, but it went straight to voicemail and he didn't return her message. She knew Josh was feeling left out and she wanted to reassure him but at the same time she was starting to feel a bit resentful of his presumed place in her life. She knew they could get their friendship back on track though as soon as she made him understand some boundaries.

She pulled up to the meeting a few minutes before it started and waved to a small group outside. They waved back half-heartedly and then turned back to their conversation. Georgia grabbed a water from the bin outside the meeting room and looked around for someone she knew. She spotted a group of women who had started coming to the meeting only a few weeks after she did and walked over to them. "Hi Karen, Bree. Hi Grace. It's great to see you guys!" Her cheery greeting was met with silence and stares until finally Grace spoke up. "Georgia. How are you?"

"I'm doing okay. Guys, what's going on? Has something happened?"

"No, Georgia, we are fine." Again it was Grace who spoke while Karen and Bree watched her. Their coldness was off-putting and Georgia didn't understand it.

The meeting started and everyone moved off to their chairs, talking among themselves, leaving Georgia standing alone. She made her way to a chair and took a seat. The meeting got under way and Georgia tried hard to shake the feeling that she had done something to offend people. She noticed a couple of people look at her and then look away quickly, not wanting to be seen. It must just be her imagination Georgia thought.

Just then, there was a disturbance behind her and turning, Georgia saw Josh enter with a couple of men from the group. They were smiling and one clapped him on the back. Karen and Bree started motioning for Josh to come sit with them and they moved over a chair to make room for him. Josh stood in the aisle and stared directly at Georgia with a cold, hard look before turning with a wounded smile to Karen. Both the women hugged him warmly and he sat between them, talking quietly as they patted his shoulder and rubbed his back.

Georgia turned back to the speaker and tried to concentrate on the meeting, but her heart wasn't in it and she was glad when the hour ended. Slipping out of her row of seats, she saw again that Josh was surrounded by Karen, Grace, Bree, and a couple of others who seemed to be protectively reassuring him. Georgia was nearly to her car when she heard her name called and turned around.

"Denise! I didn't see you come in."

Denise walked up to Georgia and gave her a quick hug. "It's good to see you Georgia. I keep meaning to call, but you know how it is."

Georgia was truly glad to see her friend and hugged her back. "What's going on around here? Is it just my imagination or are people really talking about me?"

Georgia laughed, expecting Denise to join her. But Denise looked serious and thoughtful as she took Georgia by the arm and steered her toward her own car. "If you have a minute, Georgia, we need to talk."

They settled in Denise's Camry and Georgia felt her anxiety growing. "Okay, let's talk. What's going on?"

"Georgia, you and Josh were pretty close, right? "

Georgia nodded and waited for Denise to continue.

"Well, about three weeks ago, Josh came to a meeting. He shared with the group that he was in a very vulnerable place with his grief and that someone from the group had taken advantage of him. He said that when he was really new to the meetings that an older woman had seduced him and after sleeping with him for several weeks she had gotten back together with her husband and dumped him. Georgia, he named you as the woman."

"What? He said what?" Georgia looked stunned. Her mouth opened in astonishment. "Denise! I never slept with him! I never even thought of him in that way. I wouldn't, I couldn't, I only wanted to be his friend"

Denise reached over quickly and took Georgia's hand, forcing her to focus her attention. "Georgia. I know it. I know it! And most everyone does as well. It's just a few people who like to believe the worst of people and they do talk. This will blow over."

"But it's not right." Georgia stuttered. "It's not true. How could he do this to me?"

"I know, I know. He's painted himself as a victim, someone you took advantage of and used for your own needs. It happens, Georgia, especially in self-help groups like these."

"What do I do now? What if Ryan hears this?"

"I don't know. I guess you could talk to Josh, explain how hurtful this feels. Why don't you discuss it with Ryan first and see what he thinks?"

"Thanks Denise. Thank you for being a friend and telling me about this. I do need to explain it to Ryan and then I think we'll both talk to Josh."

CHAPTER 31

JACK GOT TO THE STATION EARLY the next morning with an unexpected swing to his step. Whistling to himself, he ignored the looks of surprise from the other detectives in the squad room who were used to his no-nonsense approach. Jack hung his jacket carefully on the back of his chair and looked up to find his buddy, Joe, watching him with a strange expression on his face. "Man, what's got into you?" Joe handed Jack a cup of steaming coffee.

"Can't a guy just be in a good mood?" "Guys can. You never are." Joe joked back. "You win the lottery or something?"

"Yeah, or something." Jack inhaled the coffee aroma before taking a quick sip of the scalding liquid. He waved Joe off with a nod of thanks. He didn't quite understand how one coffee date a couple of weeks ago could still leave him in such a good mood.

When Caroline had asked him to coffee, he was surprised, but thought she just wanted to talk more about her friend. He never imagined a woman like that would be interested in just talking to him. So he had agreed to meet her the following week when he thought he might have something more to discuss about the case. It had surprised him how much he looked forward to seeing her again, and knew he was going to disappoint her when he didn't have the DNA results back yet. But the date came along and she hadn't really asked him anything about the case at all. She asked about his life and they spent nearly three hours talking.

By the time coffee was over it seemed natural that they should make a date for the following week for dinner. He would have liked to have seen her sooner, but Caroline was traveling for her work. When he finally confessed that he didn't think she would be interested in him, Caroline teased him unmercifully and good heartedly. "Wow, some detective you make, Jack Stanton. I practically threw myself at you at the station and you didn't figure it out?" Her blue eyes twinkled, daring him to defend himself.

The memory still made him smile.

He was thinking of where to go for their date when he was pulled back to the present by the plop of an envelope on his desk. Maggie stood in front of him with her hands on hip and a quizzical look.

"Jack? Jack! Where was your mind, bud? I've been standing here a full minute."

"Sorry, Mags, what do you have for me?"

"You asked me to rush this one so I wanted to get the results to you as soon as I had them. The prints from that dinner party the other day."

"Thanks, Mags."

Jack tossed the file on his desk and hung his jacket over the back of his chair. He rolled up his shirtsleeves and propping both elbows on the desk, he picked up the mug and took a sip of hot steaming coffee. This was the only time station house coffee tasted okay and over the years, Jack had come to look forward to this ritual of enjoying a sip of coffee and taking in the sights of the station from the vantage of his desk. He really loved his job and he loved this old station, no matter how many times he cussed it for the long hours and the family it had taken from him. His mind wandered back to Caroline and he thought just maybe he might have another chance if he didn't blow it again. He picked up the envelope. He had to admit, the lady was smart. He didn't really think they would find anything from her dinnerware DNA, but he did want to make her happy and he liked the way her eyes lit up when she told him about her stealthy theft of the dinner fork. His smile faded a bit when he looked at the name at the top of the report.

"Maggie," he called out just as the lab tech pushed the elevator button. "Hang on a minute, will ya?"

"What is it, Jack?"

"Are you sure you sent the right file? The one from the silver fork last week?"

"Yeah, the one you wanted me to run to impress your girlfriend. I got it right." Maggie grinned and waved as she stepped into the elevator.

Jack went back to his desk, reading the file as he walked the familiar path between desks and filing cabinets. He flipped on his computer as soon as he sat down. The name he expected to see on the report was Joshua Lehman. The name printed there was Jonathan "Johnny" Atkins.

Jack pulled up the records for Jonathan Atkins and found himself reading a long list of priors, everything from petty theft to drunken brawls. He beat up a guy so badly the guy was in the hospital but he refused to press charges. Another charge for DUI was dropped when the arresting officer was put on suspension for a separate charge. Nothing much was every proven against Atkins but there was a lot of smoke around him. The next page of priors was more troubling. Atkins had graduated from petty theft to being a suspect in carjacking ring, stealing high end automobiles for a chop shop. He had done a couple of years in prison for a burglary gone wrong. The homeowner came home early and was pistol whipped badly enough to have his jaw wired shut for three months.

After serving his time, Atkins seemed to have matured as a criminal. His list of offenses started to include more sophisticated thinking. He was charged in a series of business scams, stealing from small businesses. He had been lucky from his point of view. The judge had gone easy on him, probably due to the innocent look he had about him. It made him look much younger than his actual age. He made bail and the charges were dropped, thanks to a good attorney, probably paid for with money earned from his scams. His time in prison seemed to have only educated him on a better way to commit a crime, thought Jack.

"Hey, what are you doing looking at my guy?" Charlie's loud baritone carried across the room as he looked over Jack's shoulder.

"You know this guy?" Jack asked.

"Sure, we been looking for Atkins for a few weeks now. He's MIA. His mother was killed at the home they share and he hasn't been seen since. What are you doing with him?"

"I'm not really sure, Charlie. Is this guy a suspect in the death?"

"Aw, everybody's a suspect when we ain't got nothing. We haven't been able to find him, even for notification. He might be the perp, might not. Somebody smothered the old lady and neighbors said Johnny was home that night."

"Well, something's going on. I found this guy while I was looking for Josh Lehman. Why is he using an alias and why has he disappeared from his home the same time his mother was killed?"

"Yeah, that's a question, all right. I'll see what I can find on the latest on the old lady's case. In the meantime, though, Chief is howling about something. Says we gotta get up to his office for a meeting right now."

"Yeah, sure." Jack pushed back from his desk and headed to the elevator with Charlie, but his troubled thoughts were still centered on Johnny Atkins.

CHAPTER 32

"I COULDN'T BELIEVE IT, RYAN," Georgia fumed. "I was so angry, but I marched right back in that room and found Josh. How could he do this to me? I told him we were going to talk this thing out and get to the bottom of it tonight."

Ryan dried the plate and placed it carefully on the shelf as he listened for the second time that evening as Georgia reported on her encounter at the grief support meeting. As soon as he came home from work tonight, he knew something was wrong and he was afraid that Georgia was retreating back to her old depression, the way she had right after Kaden's death. But he had slowly coaxed the story from her and found that she wasn't depressed. She was angry. Even now her body seemed to tremble from the injustice of the lies Josh had told. Georgia was wiping the countertop with the vengeance of a survivor and Ryan thought for a minute she might wipe right through the granite top. The mental image made him want to smile. That would be a disaster right now he knew to not take her anger seriously so he quickly refocused on Georgia's words . He was just so happy to see Georgia righteously fired up about something, just like the old days.

"I told him to be here by 8:00 PM. He had better not be late."

The last sentence caught Ryan's full attention. "Wait, you told him to come here? Do you think that's the best thing, Georgia? Do we want him here after the way things turned out last time?"

"Well, I want to straighten this out and I thought it would be good for you to be here too." Georgia faltered a little as she looked up at Ryan. "You want to clear this up, don't you?"

"Honey, of course, I do." The endearment slipped out and seemed to go unnoticed by either of them. "But you and I know the truth and that's all that matters, isn't it?"

"Thank you for believing me. But I feel so betrayed by Josh. We were friends and I just think I should try to work through this with him."

Ryan slung the dishtowel over his shoulder and pushed the cabinet closed as he turned to Georgia. "Then that's what we'll do."

The evening passed quickly and at 8:00 PM sharp, the doorbell rang. Georgia looked up from her magazine and met Ryan's eye.

"Here we go." she got up to answer the door, Ryan a few steps behind her.

Josh was leaning against the door frame, hands in his pockets, when the door opened. He stared at Georgia a few seconds, assessing her mood, then saw Ryan standing behind her. He reached around Georgia and held out his hand to shake Ryan's.

"Come on in, Thanks for coming over." Ryan shook hands and pulled Josh into the room as Georgia closed the door behind them.

"Sure, not a big deal. I'm glad you're here though. I thought maybe I should bring someone with me. I don't want any misunderstandings."

"Oh Josh, for goodness sake! When did things go so off-track with us?" Georgia's frustration exploded.

Josh turned slowly and smiled at her. "I don't know what you mean. You asked me to come over and I came. Are we going to talk civilly and politely?"

"Josh, we just want to clear the air a little. Why don't you come in and sit down?" Ryan took control of the conversation and steered them into the family room with a quick look back at Georgia.

Taking a deep breath, Georgia tried to imagine what was going on with Josh and framed her words carefully. "You and I are friends. I know things have been a little tense lately, but I don't understand what has happened. I would like to talk about it with you."

Josh looked serene and confident as he stared at Georgia while she talked. Then he turned back to Ryan.

"Do you have any idea what's going on here? Georgia hasn't spoken to me since she threw me out of this house weeks ago and now she's acting like I've done something to her."

"Please speak to me, not Ryan, when I ask a question." Georgia was now calm but assured. "I didn't throw you out of the house. Your behavior was inappropriate and you were asked to leave. Now I hear stories you have been telling others at the support group that hurt my reputation, and me as well as disrespect Ryan. That's why I want to talk to you."

Josh brushed his long hair back from his eyes and leaned back into the sofa. He laughed a little. "Oh is that all? I thought this was something big. Listen, Georgia, those old ladies at that support group need a little gossip from time to time to keep them going. I didn't tell them anything. They just drew their own conclusions and I didn't correct them. I was mad at you for the way you treated me. You hurt me, Georgia, by acting like I was a danger to you."

Josh's sudden change in mood was confusing, but Georgia tried to put herself in his place and find some understanding.

"Okay, Josh, I don't want you to think I feel like you are a bad person. I don't. But letting people believe something awful about me hurts me. You can't just say nothing. Friends defend each other when it's needed. You let me down when you didn't stand up for me."

"I just don't think it's a big deal, Georgia. I'm sorry if you feel that it is. I can tell Karen to stop talking about it. She'll take care of the others."

"Well, that's a start for sure. But I would like you to do a little more than that, Josh. You need to make sure they know it's not true."

"Sure, Georgia," he was calm and answered so quietly that Georgia had trouble hearing him. "Whatever you say. I'm done with all of this."

"What do you mean that you're done?" Ryan asked from his chair across the room.

"Aw, nothing, man, except that I'm tired of this game. It's time to finish this. I think I've done about all I can do."

Georgia looked at Josh for a long minute then she got to her feet and put her hand on his shoulder. "Okay, Josh, if you're done with our friendship that's okay. I can accept that. I wish you nothing but the best. I guess there's not much else to say, but I do want to give you something before you leave. Will you wait here a minute with Ryan?"

"Yeah, sure, whatever." Josh stared straight ahead of him as Georgia gave Ryan a concerned look and left the room.

"So, Josh, come on out to the kitchen. Let's get something to drink while we wait a minute okay?"

Josh stood up and followed Ryan through the dining room. As Ryan got out glasses and filled them with ice, Josh stopped in front of a group of pictures of Kaden hanging on the way.

"That kid sure liked ice cream," He laughed.

Ryan half turned and smiled. "Yeah, she did. Mostly chocolate." He stepped in to the pantry to get the bottle of soda.

"You know, if she hadn't stopped for ice cream at the park that day, she might have missed those balloons. They nearly blew away in the wind." Josh said softly, nearly to himself.

In the pantry, Ryan stopped mid-reach for the soda bottle. His blood seemed to turn to sludge as his heart hammered in his chest. "What did you say?"

Josh appeared behind him inside the pantry. "You heard me. I nearly didn't get her because the damn wind nearly blew the balloon away." He whispered just as his hand holding the brass candlestick from the dining room table crashed onto Ryan's head. The candlestick was heavy and Josh swung it like a bat. Ryan fell to the floor, blood pouring from the wound near his temple. Josh danced away from him as Ryan, holding his head with both hands, tried to stand up and reached for him. He fell forward onto the kitchen floor.

"Now, look what you did, man, you're getting blood all over the place. Not like that little kid who just laid there in the street. You know, she never even moved." Josh kicked viciously at Ryan's ribs and felt them break as his boot connected.

"Man, it was a rush when I felt her body hit the car. I knew I had her, you know? I knew she was gone before she hit the pavement. It was her fault. It was all her fault! All my life, I had to hear about my father and his perfect little daughter. Did you know we came here one day to see her? My father never even knew her but he was so proud of her. His genes created her. He was obsessed with her." Bending over Ryan's body, spit flying from his mouth, Josh let his rage build and spill out of him.

"It took some guts for him to find her. He saved for weeks for the payoff. He even sold my bike. My bike! Just to pay some flunkie to tell him where his precious sperm went to. Then he came home one day, all excited. He found her and she was beautiful. She had the perfect life with a mother and father who loved her. She had it all. She had everything!"

He kicked at Ryan's head again and Ryan groaned.

"Just look at you. Not much left of your perfect family now is there? By the time I'm done, that wife of yours will look worse than you do. And you can't do anything to save her, can you? I want that to be your last thought, man."

Josh raised the candlestick over his head again, preparing to deliver the fatal blow to Ryan's head.

"Josh." Georgia's voice was low and calm as he turned to her. "Maybe I don't need saving."

She squeezed the trigger.

CHAPTER 33

THREE HOURS AFTER THE CORONER had pronounced Josh, the house was still full of people. Crime scene tape was wrapped around the outside driveway to keep the curious at bay. Ryan had been taken by ambulance to the hospital for treatment of a concussion and Georgia sat in the living room, once again, being interviewed by Detective Stanton. She was wrapped in a blanket because even though the temperature was balmy she couldn't seem to get warm. But her hands were steady and her voice was assured as she answered questions.

"So, you bought the gun after you and your husband separated?"

"Yes, I wanted to feel safe being here alone. I took a few lessons at the gun range."

"You had invited Josh over to talk?"

"Yes, I had heard some disturbing stories he was spreading about me and I wanted to talk to him."

"What were the stories?"

Georgia looked down at her hands, clasped in front of her. "He told people that we were having an affair. Or, I guess, more correctly that I had seduced him."

"And that wasn't true?"

"Of course not! We were friends and that's all. Nothing else even occurred to me. I wanted to talk to him to clear things up and get him to stop spreading rumors about me. Then I was going to give him a picture taken of us just before he left. I went upstairs to get it then remembered that it was in the study so I came back downstairs. That's when I heard a noise in the kitchen. I started to go see about it when I saw Josh pull Ryan from the pantry into the kitchen. He had the bloody candlestick in his other hand. The gun was in the desk in the study so I just went and got it."

"Okay, then what?"

Georgia started to shake and she rocked back and forth. "I heard him. I heard him threaten Ryan and me. And I heard" She stopped for a minute as tears sprang to her eyes. "I heard him talk about Kaden. He said she was the reason he had such a bad life and he said that he killed her."

Georgia cried silently for a minute the continued with her story. "I shot him. I just had to stop him. He would have killed Ryan. I didn't even think about it, I just did it. And I would do it again." She looked up defiantly as her shoulders straightened. "I would do it again. That's when the phone rang. It was you. Why were you calling me this late at night?"

"I had just found some information today about Josh. I called you to warn you about him."

Georgia gave a rueful laugh and then looked guiltily at Jack as he continued.

"I ran some DNA obtained from your friend Caroline and found that Josh was actually a man named John Atkins. He was a 31 year old career criminal and it raised a lot of concern. Caroline, Ms. Richter, felt he was insinuating himself into your life and she asked me to check it out. Turns out her instincts were good." Jack couldn't help but feel a little proud of that and he fumbled a bit with his notes.

"Thirty one? He looked a lot younger. I can't believe I was so naïve and gullible. I just wanted so badly to have a friend and Josh fit into that vacuum in my life so easily. I guess that's what he intended. But why would he? He said he killed Kaden."

"We're just starting that part of the investigation but we have found some papers at the apartment Josh was renting. It was filled with high end electronics and jewelry. Apparently he pawned them as needed for cash. He also had photos of you and your daughter. He was stalking you long before Kaden's death. I guess he had some kind of obsession with you or with her. We'll know more as things progress."

Jack folded his notebook and stood. "You know we can do more later, Mrs. Maxwell. I think we have enough to start. You want me to call someone?"

Georgia pulled herself together and answered "Yes, my friend. Caroline."

She never noticed that Jack pulled Caroline's phone number from the speed dial on his phone.

CHAPTER 33

THREE DAYS LATER, GEORGIA stepped into the hospital room expecting to see Ryan lying in the bed as he had been since the accident. She had spent every day at the hospital as Ryan recovered. He was scheduled to be released today but they still had not talked about their future. He was standing by the window, dressed and ready to go. Georgia walked up to stand beside him and he silently reached out for her hand.

"How are you feeling? Do you feel steady enough to stand? That's quite a bump you have on your head." she asked after a minute.

"I'm fine. How are you?" Ryan turned to her with concern on his face. "It's been a tough few days."

Georgia sat on the edge of the hospital bed and faced him. "You know, I think I'm okay, Ryan. I killed a person. That doesn't feel right. But he's the person who took the most important thing in our world away from us. And he wanted to take you away from me too. So I can't dwell on it too much."

"I understand. I just wish I had seen it sooner. I should have been the one."

"No, don't even think that. I was the one who was completely taken in by Josh, I mean Johnny. It's still hard to think of him by that name. Apparently he's the lead suspect in his mother's death too." Georgia shuddered. "Just thinking about what might have happened and how close we came to losing everything all over again. Thank God, Caroline was suspicious enough to question things when I was too blinded by grief to see straight. She's the one who started seeing that things weren't right."

"Caroline is a good friend, Georgia. To both of us. I hope she knows how much she has done for us."

"I think she knows. She loves us." Taking a deep breath, Georgia continued "Ryan, I can't help but feel guilty to a great degree for this. If I hadn't gone to that clinic in the first place and then lied about it this would never have happened. If I had only been honest with you and we had been together on this, Kaden might still be with us."

"I agree that you should have been honest with me but I don't know if that would have saved Kaden. There's no way you could ever imagine something like this happening. Georgia, he targeted her out of hatred and a misguided idea that he would hurt his father by hurting her. That wouldn't have changed. He would still have felt that way."

Ryan came to the bedside and put his hands lightly on Georgia's shoulders. He leaned in gently and kissed her softly on the mouth. "But from now on we have to be a team. We have to be honest with each other. You know that we still have some work to do right?" Georgia nodded, her mouth still tingling from the pressure of his.

"But I want to come home, Georgia. I mean really come home. I want us to work. I want us to be a family again. Is that going to be okay?"

Georgia stood and put her arms around Ryan, pulling him close to her. "Yes, it's more than okay. And I promise that I have changed. Ryan. No more secrets and no more lies. I want those things too. Let's go home and I'll cook dinner for us. Then let's talk about how we start over. There's just one thing I want to do first."

"Okay."

"I stopped for some flowers on the way over. I thought we should visit Kaden together before we go home."

* * *

99285729R00092

Made in the USA
Lexington, KY
14 September 2018